The Treasure of the sun God

A Conjurer of Rhodes, Book 3

Jack Massa

Published by
Triskelion Books
www.triskelionbooks.com

ISBN 978-0-9976461-5-3

Print Edition published January, 2019

Cover design by Mirna Gilman, BooksGoSocial.

In Memoriam

Andrew Salvatore Massa
(1920 - 2002)

I have known
no better father,
no better man

The one Greek power that preserved complete and genuine independence in Hellenistic times ... was the maritime republic of Rhodes. Rhodian wealth came primarily from her extensive carrying trade...

As a result of this heavy and widespread maritime commerce, Rhodes also had a natural vested interest in the suppression of piracy.

—Peter Green
Alexander to Actium

Rhodes is an island in the sea ... On this island stands a colossus, one hundred and twenty feet high, the image of the sun god. The artist who built it used so much bronze as seemed likely to create a shortage in the mines. For the casting of this statue involved the bronze industry of the whole world ...

... Little by little he reached the goal of his dream. With incredible boldness, he created a god similar to the real god, and gave a second Sun to the world.

—Philo of Byzantium
On the Seven Wonders of the World
circa 225 BCE

The Story So Far

As told in A Conjurer of Rhodes, Book 1 and 2.

On the Greek island of Rhodes, a young man named Korax recklessly dabbles in magic. He conjures the God Dionysus to help him win a singing contest and humiliate his enemies. Next day, the enraged young men corner him on the street and smash his skull. Only the witchcraft of Korax's mother brings him back from death. But even as his wound heals, his mind remains damaged. In hope of curing him, his parents send him by sea to Thrace, the home of his mother's people. En route, the ship is captured by pirates, and Korax is sold into slavery.

He is purchased by an Egyptian high priest and spends two years as a scribe in a temple on the Nile. As his wits and memories return, Korax gains initiation into the Egyptian mysteries. Guided by the Goddess Isis, he begins a serious study of magic.

Escaping the temple, he travels to Alexandria. There he joins a society of scholars and magicians from many lands. He falls in love with Kalyssa, a priestess and wife to the ambassador from Carthage. But Kalyssa's first loyalty is to her city, and she entangles Korax in a plot to murder Ptolemy, the Greek king of Egypt. Korax manages to thwart the plot and sails from Alexandria. With him is Leukon, a Celtic warrior and mercenary, now a slave whom Korax has purchased as a body guard.

After five years, Korax returns to Rhodes—uncertain of what awaits him ...

Cast of Characters

Korax - A wanderer and student of the magic arts. Returning home to Rhodes.

Leukon - A Celtic warrior. Korax's slave and bodyguard.

Korax's family

Leontes - Korax's father, an invalid.

Anticleia (deceased) - Korax's mother, a witch.

Zeno - Korax's uncle. Brother and business partner to Leontes.

Callipatria - Zeno's wife.

Isochomachus - Zeno's son, a ship captain.

Phaenna - Zeno's daughter.

Leochares - Phaenna's husband, a farmer.

Autolycus, Carya, Damagetus - Phaenna's children.

Callias (deceased) - Brother to Leontes and Zeno.

Epiteleia - Widow of Callias.

Amynias - Epiteleia's younger son, a prosperous banker.

Hegestratus - Epiteleia's elder son, a ship captain.

Servants in Zeno's house

Phoemio - A Phoenician, formerly Korax's pedagogue.

Kleis - A maid servant.

Menas - The steward, a treacherous rogue.

Glauke - A cook.

Contemporaries of Korax

Patrollos - Son of the House of Philophron, a young naval commander.

Cimon - Cousin to Patrollos, a naval officer.

Lyceas - A banker's son, business partner to Amynias.

Staphylus - A lawyer and poet, Korax's friend.

Berenicia - Priestess of Aphrodite, a courtesan and patroness of the arts.

Thalia - Daughter of the House of Philophron, Patrollos' sister.

Others

Halitherses - Father to Patrollos and Thalia, sire of the House of Philophron.

Choronice - Wife to Halitherses.

Agesilaus - Younger brother to Patrollus and Thalia.

Hicesius - An accountant, employed by Amynias.

Eriphon - Amynias' gatekeeper.

Agesandros - A magistrate, father of Staphylus.

Theadetus - A banker, father of Lyceas.

Neshicles - A physician.

Nicocles - Admiral in the Rhodian Navy.

Bolocrates - Agent and courier for the Cretan pirates.

Olbius - A pirate chieftain.

Chapter One

*O*ne day the gods of Olympus divided all the cities and lands of the Earth among themselves, each choosing their places of patronage. But since it was daytime, Helios the sun god was away from Olympus, driving his chariot across the sky. When he returned at dusk, his fellow immortals admitted, with some embarrassment, that they had forgotten to apportion him a share.

"I am content," the sun god answered, "if you will grant me that one island, newly risen from the sea." And he pointed his blazing spear to a place off the coast where Rhodes was just then emerging from the waves.

The Olympians agreed of course. How could they not? But afterward, some poets hinted, certain of the gods regretted how matters had fallen out—seeing how balmy and agreeable was the island they had ceded to Helios. This was said in particular of Poseidon, the jealous god of the sea and bringer of earthquakes.

Korax recounted this story to Leukon the night before they landed in Rhodos, the island's capital. They sat together under the stars, their backs to the rail of the freighter, sharing the last of a nearly empty wineskin.

"So your island is home to the sun god," Leukon remarked thoughtfully. "Does he keep his treasure there?"

"In a manner of speaking," Korax answered, thinking of the vast sums of gold and silver held in the treasury at the Temple of Helios.

Leukon grunted and took on a distant, morose expression. Korax knew that visage well. Over the course of the voyage from Alexandria, he had seen it often. The Celt was possessed of a volatile temperament. His moods soared and plunged precipitously, from childlike elation to dismal brooding, with no discernible cause.

Leukon had proven himself much more than the brash barbarian Korax first supposed. For one thing, the man owned a powerful intellect. He spoke *koine,* the Greek trading tongue, fluently, and also had a smattering of Macedonian and Egyptian. In their first days at sea, he examined Korax's books and expressed an interest in learning to read them. Korax started him where Greek schoolboys started, with Homer. The Celt learned quickly. Korax gathered that the man's mind had been developed by years of oral teaching. The lore of the Celts was transmitted by spoken recitation, and Leukon had absorbed vast amounts of poetry. His conversation also revealed extensive knowledge of the forests and rivers of Europe, tree and herb lore, his tribe's genealogy, and the epic tales of his people.

But as for his own history, he kept silent. "I've not proven worthy of having my tale told," was all he would say. That was when the grim, impenetrable mask would descend, and no amount of probing would elicit further talk.

Korax climbed to his feet. Leaving the Celt to his brooding, he wandered to the foredeck and looked out over the dark, quiet sea. In the starlight, Rhodes formed a low shadow on the horizon. The captain had heaved to at dusk within sight of the island, leaving the tricky approach into the harbor for daylight.

Staring at his homeland, Korax wondered what he would find there. For him, the voyage had also been a time of brooding— reflecting with sorrow over what he had lost in Alexandria, worrying over what might await him in Rhodes.

More and more, he dwelled on the memories that had returned to him in his last months in Alexandria. Sometimes the recollections came in dreams, sometimes in reveries as he lay on the deck and stared at the open sky.

Vividly, he saw his mother, sitting over him night after night, healing his grievous wound by pouring her magic into his body. Toward the end, she looked frail and weak. His body had recovered, though he was still plagued by dizzy spells. And his mind was still damaged—distracted and confused. One day, his father came and told him his mother was ill. On her insistence, they were sending Korax away on a ship, to visit her family in Thrace. She no longer had the strength to care for her injured son, but she believed strongly that his best chance for recovering was to leave Rhodes and go to her people.

Korax had boarded one of the family's trading vessels, accompanied by Phoemio, his servant and pedagogue since his childhood. Phoemio was a Phoenician, a humorous and talkative man, completely devoted to his young master. Day after day, Korax paced the decks of the freighter, with Phoemio following close behind, anxious that a sudden swell or bout of dizziness might cause the young man to fall overboard.

In one terrifying memory, Korax stood on the foredeck and spied a squadron of hemiolias—Cretan pirate vessels. Apparently, he'd been captured by the Cretans and held for ransom. In later fragments, he recalled a feast hall filled with rough, bearded men and somber women garbed in black. Oddly, he played the lyre for them, and recited poetry.

Then one night a messenger arrived. The pirate chieftain, a wily rogue named Olbius, informed Korax that the ransom had not been paid. The young Rhodian was seized and put in shackles. Next day, he was on a slave ship bound for Alexandria.

Why had the ransom not come? Had the money been lost in transit? Had the family fortunes suddenly turned so they could not afford the price? Both possibilities seemed highly doubtful, yet the question remained ...

More than five years had passed since he left home. He had departed with a bandaged head and a mind swimming in madness. He had lived as a wretched slave and as a favored guest in a palace. He had loved and lost his love. He had served priests, diplomats, and a king; contested with men and magicians—even with a god. He had been cured of his madness, only to nearly bring madness back on himself by drinking too deeply at the fountain of magic.

Yes, he ought never to have attempted the rituals to draw down the power of the sun god, he saw that now in hindsight. The dazzling might of Helios was more than he could absorb at his current stage of development. Korax had rolled up that book, vowed not to open it again until some future time when, as his master Amasis intended, he had grown very wise and exhausted all other magical lore.

He was lucky to have survived those rites with his mind intact. It had taken months, but diligent practice of the mental regimens of Egypt had finally brought him back into balance. The energy of the god had settled, leaving Korax the man master of himself.

But who was Korax the man?

Inwardly he felt spiritless, vacant. All his work and study seemed to have accomplished nothing—nothing except to lead him to this place of blank potential, as void of character and detail as the shadowy coast of Rhodes on the horizon. He appeared to himself now like a bow, newly fashioned and newly strung.

But where was the arrow? And who was the archer?

Chapter Two

The Colossus of Helios towered over Rhodos, four times higher than the highest roof. Korax and Leukon stood at the forward rail, watching the gold giant draw near as their ship crossed the harbor.

For once, the Celt was frankly overawed. "That is truly a god standing on the earth," he marveled.

Korax smiled, pleased at the man's amazement. Beyond the docks and harbor walls, the city climbed a broad hill, an orderly mosaic of white facades, red roofs, and green gardens. In the brilliant sunlight of late spring, Rhodos looked even more beautiful than he remembered.

The crewmen reefed sail as the freighter glided toward the docks. With hawsers and stout boathooks, a team of stevedores guided the vessel into an empty slip. Planks were lowered, and the sailors scrambled down onto the landing. Korax joined them in speaking prayers and pouring libations into the water, homage to Poseidon in gratitude for their safe voyage.

By arrangement, Korax left most of his gear on board. He would return later with porters and pay the captain the balance he owed. Now he took his sword and his satchel, with the money-bags inside, and left the ship.

Leukon accompanied him along the busy docks. Even among travelers from many nations, the Celt drew attention. His giant shoulders and drooping mustache attracted glances of surprise and fascination, while the long sword at his hip made a more fearful impression.

Anxious to see his family, Korax took the shortest route across the lower city. This brought them past the great temples and through the Square of the Colossus. Beyond the Temple of Helios, they traversed the narrow streets of a tradesmen's warren. To Korax, it all seemed hauntingly familiar. Yet he also felt an obscure difference, as if something were missing from the city. Pondering this impression, he was reminded of what Apollonius the poet had told him in Alexandra—that the sparkle of optimism had departed from Rhodes.

At midmorning, they reached the street where his father's house stood—the house where he had grown up. In Egypt, as his memories filtered back to him, Korax had sometimes been tormented by doubts—not fully certain that these memories of Rhodes were not delusions born of his madness. Now, seeing the street and the house as he remembered them, he experienced a deep sense of relief.

He marched up resolutely and knocked on the thick wooden door. When no response came after a few moments, he pounded impatiently with a balled fist.

Finally the door was opened by a scrawny little man Korax did not recognize. The gatekeeper frowned at him, then arched his brows and swayed back on seeing the Celt.

"What is your business?"

"I am here to see your master, Leontes," Korax said.

"Sorry, you have the wrong house." The door started to shut.

No. It could not be! Seized by panic, Korax almost let the door close. At the last instant, he braced it open with the flat of his hand. "Wait! Leontes the merchant, I *know* this to be his house."

The gatekeeper shook his head. "Not anymore. This house belongs to his nephew, Amynias."

Stunned, Korax recalled Amynias, the cousin he knew—and hated. The door had almost closed again. He shoved it back forcefully.

"Since when is Amynias master here? And where is Leontes?"

The slave gaped in exasperation. "My master Amynias purchased the house from Leontes four years ago. Leontes is a poor invalid now and lives at the house of his brother Zeno. If you follow this avenue till it turns up the hill, then continue ..."

"I know Zeno's house," Korax snapped. He turned away and stalked up the street.

Leukon loped after him. "Your father has lost his house. This sounds like ill news."

"So it would appear," Korax answered through closed teeth.

Bad enough that the house Korax grew up in should be lost. But that it belonged now to his cousin Amynias seemed to turn the misfortune into an insult. It reminded him of all the insults he had suffered at the hands of Amynias, Patrollos, and their clique. It brought back that wet, gray morning five years ago when they attacked him and broke his head.

Korax had long ago put aside any thirst for revenge. During his years of spiritual discipline, he had come to recognize that he bore a share of the blame. His merciless taunting had goaded Patrollos and his cohorts beyond their endurance. By his own arrogance and vindictiveness, Korax had brought the disaster on himself. He didn't know how Patrollos and the others would respond to his return. But for his part, he planned to keep a wary distance from them and stir up no further trouble.

So he was surprised now to find the old resentment and animosity boiling to the surface. He needed to leave all that in the past, to forget the childish feud. He had returned to help his family and, if possible, to be of service to Rhodes. That was his charge from the goddess Athene.

He reached the neighborhood where Zeno's mansion stood. Zeno was his father's brother and business partner. Korax remembered him as a fond uncle, and his wife, Callipatria, as a loving aunt. With Leukon on his heels, he walked up and pounded on the gate.

Presently the door creaked open. Korax's eyes widened when he saw the gatekeeper. The face was older, with drawn cheeks and lines around the eyes, but Korax recognized Phoemio at once.

"Yes...?" Phoemio peered at him, then gave a start, his mouth falling open.

"You've acquired a few gray hairs," Korax observed.

"Master Korax?" Phoemio leaned unsteadily on the gate.

Korax embraced him. Phoemio moaned loudly and broke into sobs. His sank to his knees, clutching Korax by the legs.

"Come, Phoemio. Stand." Korax's voice was choked.

Several moments passed before Phoemio managed to rise. "But how is this possible? All these years! Where have you been?"

"I'll tell you all later. Is my father here?"

"Yes. Yes, of course."

Phoemio ushered him through the gate, then gaped at Leukon. "But master, who is this terrible giant who shadows you?"

Korax placed a hand on the Celt's muscular arm. "He is Leukon, my servant and friend. Treat him well, Phoemio, for he's saved my life, even as you once did."

"He is welcome then." Phoemio scanned the tall warrior with a dubious eye. "But he'll need to bow his head to pass through some of the doorways."

They entered the broad courtyard, bordered on three sides by columns of pearly marble. The spacious house seemed nearly deserted, with unswept tiles and withered vines clinging to the stonework.

Korax looked about glumly. "Where is everyone, Phoemio?"

"Oh, master Zeno is in the town, and the mistress is likely in her weaving room. I will tell her you are here, after I take you to your father."

"But the servants, the gardener ... It all seems so quiet."

Phoemio frowned and lowered his voice. "There aren't as many servants as in former days. Master Zeno had to sell some of his household to pay the family's debts. I myself am still here only because I'm the one person with patience enough to attend your father. Times have been hard in Rhodes, especially the past two years." Phoemio wiped his eye. "But I'm certain things will get better now that you are home."

Leaving Leukon to wait by the fountain, Korax followed Phoemio into the main foyer and up the grand staircase. Pedestals and niches, once occupied by statues and expensive vases, now stood empty.

"How is my father?" Korax asked, as they walked quickly down the upstairs hall.

Phoemio shook his head ruefully. "He has not been well since ..." He halted, a new expression of anguish appearing. "Oh, master, forgive me. I did not think to tell you. Your mother, she—"

"I know, Phoemio. She is dead."

"But how did you learn ...?"

"Later. Please, tell me about my father."

"Yes, I'm sorry." Phoemio's hand pressed his forehead. "So much has happened. When I returned from Crete with your letter, your father was sorely distressed, mourning the loss of your mother. He carried on bravely, but after he had sent the ransom and you did not return, his health just collapsed."

So the ransom had been paid, Korax thought. Then why had it never arrived in Crete? He brushed the question aside to concentrate on what Phoemio was saying.

"...He was deathly ill all that winter. A disease clouded his eyes until he could barely see. Of course, he could no longer work. Still, he refused to abandon his house. But eventually he had no choice, and Zeno brought him here to live. Now he sits all day staring at the sky. The whole world is a dim blur in his sight. He barely speaks to anyone. I hope your return will brighten his spirits. I know it will."

They had reached the door to Leontes' chamber. Phoemio held it open, then followed Korax inside.

Despite the open balcony, the room contained a damp odor of sickness. Korax's father lay on a couch, pale and withered, with unshaved beard and white hair long and wild. Stepping near, Korax saw a milky film covering both of the old man's eyes. With a twinge he recalled the tale of Phineas, the blind seer cursed by the gods.

"Master Leontes," Phoemio said quietly. "Here is wonderful news. Your son has returned to us. Master Korax, he is here."

For a moment, Leontes did not react. Then his head shuddered and he scowled. "What nonsense are you speaking Phoemio? Go away. Leave me in peace."

"Father." Korax knelt and touched the old man's arm.

Leontes flinched. "Leave me, I say!"

"Father, it is Korax. Do not turn from me, please. I have been gone from Rhodes for five years. I was taken by pirates, but now I have returned."

Leontes' pale lips parted and a look of unspeakable misery passed over his face. Then the angry scowl descended again.

"Lying slaves! Why do you torment an old man with your tricks? My son is dead, and justly so. He caused the death of my dear wife with his foolishness. The gods have taken everything from me. At least leave me to suffer in peace."

Korax drew back his hands, stricken. It took him some moments to regain his composure. "You are right, father. My heedless actions brought about my mother's death. I am terribly sorry for that, and for all the sorrow I've caused you."

Leontes stared at the daylight, blank and immobile as a frieze.

"But I have returned to make amends," Korax stammered. "I will do whatever I can to ease your suffering. And if the day comes when you can put aside your grief and embrace me as your son, I will be here waiting."

The old man's head twitched, but that was his only response. Korax climbed to his feet and left the chamber, Phoemio on his heels.

Chapter Three

I t must have been a shock for your father," Callipatria said. "He had given up on your ever coming home—we all had. I am sure he will welcome you with an open heart once he's had time to adjust."

"Of course he will," Zeno grunted. "It would be unnatural otherwise. He will come around."

Korax had returned to the harbor with Leukon, hired a cart, and brought his belongings up to the house. Now, bathed and wearing fresh garments, he dined with his aunt and uncle on their upstairs terrace. Beyond the balustrade spread the glorious view of Rhodos and the sea that he remembered, flushed in the gold light of late afternoon.

In honor of Korax's return, Zeno had opened an amphora of wine from Thassos and ordered a lamb from the butcher shop—a delicacy rarely enjoyed except on festival days. Phoemio and the other house slaves hovered in the background, curious to observe the young master and hear his story.

"He has a right to blame me," Korax muttered. "I brought the injury on myself, and restoring my health cost my mother too much. It ... drained her." In fact, Korax knew, his mother had poured out her own life essence to save him from death. But he would not discuss the details of her magic with his aunt and uncle.

Callipatria leaned across the table to touch his wrist. "Do not blame yourself. We all make mistakes, especially when we're young. But you always had a good heart, Korax. I'm certain you never meant to harm anyone."

His aunt had not changed at all: still warm and cheerful, boundless and indiscriminate in her loving kindness. In middle age she was still lovely, full-figured, with a round face and dark, lustrous eyes. She was dressed for the occasion in a gray gown, her black hair pinned up with copper combs.

"I only hope I can make amends," Korax said, "and ease some of my father's grief." He glanced at Zeno. "I'm sure it has been difficult for you to manage affairs without his help."

"That's true enough," Zeno grumbled over his cup. He seemed to have aged more than his wife, his weathered face more wrinkled, his hair and beard showing more gray. "I don't have the brain for balancing accounts. Isochomachus helps me some in the winter, but during the season we need him at sea. That leaves the juggling of the books to my sorry wits."

Korax had been told Zeno's son was away on a trading expedition. He had been glad to hear Isochomachus was still alive and hearty. This brought to mind his other cousins. "What about Hegestratus and Amynias? Are they also captaining ships?"

"Hegestratus is, but not for us." A roughness entered Zeno's voice. "We are no longer in business with Epiteleia and her sons. After it became clear your father was not going to recover, they decided it was in their interest to split from us. It took a nasty court case to divide up the business. We finally had to pay them much more than they were owed, just to keep the lawyers' fees from bleeding us white."

Plainly, it hurt Zeno to recall these events. Korax perceived it was not only the financial losses, but the betrayal by family that had wounded his uncle. Epiteleia was the widow of Callias, the third brother who, along with Leontes and Zeno, had founded the shipping business.

"Is that how Amynias ended up owning my father's house?"

Zeno stood at the krater and ladled more wine into his cup. "No, that happened earlier. We sold him the house after moving your father here. It made no sense to keep up two houses, and we needed the money. We'd already suffered two disastrous trading seasons."

Korax was puzzled. "But how did Amynias have enough money to buy the house?"

"He is a banker now." Zeno settled back on his couch. "His friends among the ruling families set him up and made him a partner. Oh, Amynias is doing quite well. While the shippers of Rhodes have suffered, the bankers have not done badly. They simply raise their rates each year and foreclose on properties when the shippers can't pay. Amynias holds a mortgage on this house, too. I pay him interest every month."

Korax pushed away his platter. His appetite had fled. "Listen, uncle: I can help you with the business. I've had experience with accounts and documents on my travels, and I learn quickly. Also, I've brought some money home with me—a little over 4,000 Egyptian drachmas. I know it's not much, but it's yours for whatever you need."

Zeno and Callipatria both smiled fondly.

"You are a good son and nephew," Zeno said. "But we'll talk about that tomorrow. Now we want to hear all about your adventures."

"Yes!" Phoemio whispered, loud enough to be heard.

The other slaves let out a murmur of anticipation and edged closer. Zeno chuckled and waved for them all to come near. They pulled up an empty couch and stools and sat down to listen.

Korax began with what he remembered of his voyage from Rhodes and his capture by the Cretan pirates. Zeno confirmed what Phoemio had said earlier, that the ransom had been promptly paid. So it remained a mystery why the brigands had decided to sell him into bondage. Perhaps the ransom had been stolen along the way, Zeno suggested, one group of thieves betraying another. It was unusual for hostages not to be returned, but sadly it did happen. Korax agreed this was the most likely explanation—though a nagging intuition told him something else had occurred.

As he continued his tale, he deemed it prudent to leave out certain segments, particularly those concerning magic. He related only that he had become a scribe in Memphis, and eventually earned his freedom. He narrated how he had spent time in Alexandria as a student and musician, before earning enough money to sail for home.

"And you say you wrote to us, to your parents I mean," Callipatria said.

"Yes, as soon as I was able. I did not want them to think I had perished. I sent several letters, over a number of months. That would have been two and three years ago. I cannot explain why none of them arrived."

"It seems very unlucky. But then the seas have not been kind to us these past years." Zeno gave a tired, fatalistic shrug. "What about your barbarian giant? You haven't told us how you came to own him."

Korax took a long sip of the ruddy wine. "Well, I became involved in some risky ventures in Alexandria—which I'll tell you about some other time. This work required that I have the services of an able bodyguard. But don't worry about Leukon. He is a fearsome fighter but otherwise quite tame. An intelligent man, too; he's learning to read Homer."

"A Celtic Atlas with a taste for literature!" Zeno laughed at the absurdity. "You always did have a knack for attracting the unusual, Korax."

A while later, Leukon sat on a doorstep in the narrow courtyard outside the kitchen. With the other slaves of the house, he dined on leftovers from the master's table—roast lamb, figs, olives, pears, and bread.

"This lamb is delicious and most welcome," Leukon grunted. "To be honest, I find the diet of you Greeks sorely lacking in meat. I'll have more, if you don't mind."

He held out his platter to Glauke, the red-faced cook. But the stout old woman shook her head sourly. "The carcass is scraped clean. Besides, you've had three portions already. I've never seen a man eat so much."

"I've never seen so large a man," said Kleis, the young woman who cleaned the upstairs rooms. Kleis, herself a tall person, seemed impressed with the Celt's physique.

"It's still unfair that he consume three times more meat than everyone else," remarked Menas, a crabbed man of middle-age who served as Zeno's steward. "How will the household support him and his master? Two more mouths to feed, and they might as well be seven with this one's appetite."

"Master Korax is not without funds," Phoemio retorted. "He brought considerable wealth from Egypt. He and his bodyguard will not be a burden."

"I'll have some more wine then." Leukon held out his tumbler.

"I'll get it for you," Kleis volunteered.

"Thank you, sweet young lady." The Celt grinned. "These cups you use are so small. They hardly hold a single swallow."

"Our cups are perfectly adequate for normal-size mouths," Glauke replied haughtily.

"That brings to mind a question I've often wondered about," Phoemio ventured. "Pardon my asking, Leukon, and please don't take offense. But is it true that among your tribes, you decapitate your enemies and use their skulls as drinking cups?"

A collective gasp passed around the small circle.

"What nonsense," Menas said.

"Actually, it is the truth," Leukon noted learnedly. "We take the heads of slain enemies and hang them on our doorposts to do them honor. And, if an enemy is a great hero, it's common to have his skull varnished and made into a ceremonial cup. This bestows special honor on his spirit in the Otherworld."

"Such honors I would happily decline," Phoemio said. "The thought of an enemy's lips sipping from my dead skull seems small comfort to me."

Leukon grinned as Kleis returned with his replenished tumbler. "Oh, you would never have to worry about that, Phoemio. Even if you were killed in battle, my kin would not use a skull such as yours for a cup. No, the shape is all wrong—too shallow and bumpy. The best we might do is make you into a dipper for water, or possibly a ladle for stew."

A macabre quiet settled over the courtyard.

"Hah! I am jesting with you," the Celt roared. He shook his head at the gullibility of the Greeks.

Kleis giggled, and presently Phoemio added a nervous laugh. Glauke and Menas pouted sullenly.

Leukon guzzled the wine and smacked his lips. "Since there is no more meat, I'll take some more bread and olives, and another one of those sweet pears."

Korax's luggage had been carried to an unused bedroom next to the one occupied by Leontes. The chamber was large and luxurious, though at present sparsely furnished. Paneled frescoes covered the high walls, dim and shadowy in the lamp glow. The air smelled stale and musty.

Korax opened the balcony doors. A pleasant evening had settled over Rhodos, a bright half-moon gliding in the sky. He turned back into the room and began unpacking. After sorting clothes from two chests, he found his magical implements and the electrum statuette of Athene.

He took the figure from its wrapping and shined it with a cloth. He set the goddess on a low table, then made an altar by arranging white tapers and a censor. He lit the candles and added a cake of incense. He placed a small rug before the altar, sat down, and crossed his legs.

When he had meditated for a time, he felt the goddess entering the room.

"I am pleased to find you safely arrived in Rhodes."

"Yes," Korax answered. "I give thanks to you and to Poseidon. But I am pained by what I've found here."

"I advised you that your family had troubles."

"Yes, but I did not expect to find my father so ill, and for him to refuse to recognize me. His words cut me deeply."

"Because you feel his accusations are true?"

"I know they are."

"No, Korax. As I told you before, you are not to blame for your mother's death. That was the choice she made, because she loved you. Do not take your father's bitterness into your heart. His spirit has been crushed by his afflictions. But if you stand by him now, he may heal himself in time."

"I will stand by him. I pledge it on my honor." Korax took a long breath. "The money problems run deep—deeper than Zeno is letting on, I can sense it. But apart from helping him manage affairs, I'm not sure what I can do."

"You can use your arts," Athene said. "When your mother was alive, she lent her influence over all the family's ventures. She blessed the contracts and guided and protected the ships. She has left you that role. It is part of her legacy."

As the goddess spoke, an image of how to accomplish what she described formed itself in Korax's mind. "I see. I will do the workings as you suggest."

He sat quietly, pondering.

"Something else troubles you," Athene observed.

"Mysteries that are still unsolved. Today I learned for certain that my father sent my ransom to Crete. But why it never arrived remains unknown. And the letters I sent from Egypt—not a single one reached its destination. That seems beyond bad luck."

"Can you remember when you sent the letters?"

"Of course. I acted with diligent care. I paid each of the captains well and instructed them to deliver the letters in person. I gave explicit directions for finding my father's house—"

Korax's eyes popped open in the shadowy chamber. "I sent them to my father's house, but my father no longer lived there."

By then, Amynias owned the house. Was it possible Amynias had received the letters and concealed them? But why?

"Now examine the question of the ransom," Athene prompted.

Korax emptied his mind and let the impressions flow in: darkness, drifting black clouds, a hand moving. He strained to see the owner of the hand ... Amynias again!

Amynias, Patrollos, and the others—somehow they had arranged for his ransom to go astray. That might explain why Amynias would later destroy Korax's letters—to conceal the fact that Korax was alive and free, to discourage him from returning to Rhodes. Was it possible? Could his cousin's hatred really run so deep? Or was Korax's own animosity causing erroneous perceptions?

"Your vision is not wrong," Athene said. "But heed me, Korax. Do not seek revenge against Amynias and his comrades. You have rightly perceived that you own some of the blame for the crimes they committed against you. Wisdom requires you to put aside your hate."

"But if they really did this ... to strike at me in anger is one thing, but this—It is monstrous. They took away my very life. They robbed my poor father of his only living son." Dire thoughts slithered into his mind. With magic he could find out for certain the roles played by Amynias, Patrollos, and the rest. He could punish them in terrible ways.

"You have the power to do that," Athene agreed. "But if you use magic for hateful ends, then hate will flourish in your soul. Soon, it will become your master."

"What would you have me do, goddess, forgive them?" It seemed unthinkable.

"Perhaps, in time. For now, I advise you to wait and be on your guard. Let Amynias and the others weave their own fates. Stand ready to defend yourself, but nothing more. I can help protect you, but not if you stir up violence. I urge you to heed this advice, Korax. I am speaking for your good."

He withdrew into meditation, finding the place of spiritual peace. From there, he observed his rancor, writhing like a black flame.

Athene insisted he must let it go. Once before, he had spurned the advice of an immortal ally—to his later regret. With duty to his father and family to consider, he must not repeat that mistake.

"Clear-eyed goddess, I will be guided by your wisdom."

Chapter Four

Lyceas strolled along a path of hard-packed sand, through the shade of tall cypresses. He was naked, his hard-muscled form glistening with oil. Ahead, at the edge of a sunny lawn, he spotted his friend Amynias.

As Lyceas approached, Amynias hefted a bronze javelin in his hand and eyed distant targets. Bales of painted straw stood across the lawn, arranged to mimic the ranks of an advancing army. Amynias lifted the spear behind his shoulder, skipped forward and flung. His foot skidded across the foul line and the javelin arced through the cloudless sky. The point stuck in the grass, several yards short of the nearest target.

"You're off-stride today," Lyceas said. "Your shoulder's dipping. Also, you overstepped the line."

Amynias turned on him with sour irritation. Instinctively, Lyceas shrank back.

"I've had some perplexing news," Amynias confided. "Come. I'll tell you about it while we loosen up."

Lyceas followed him back along the path toward the gymnasium's high portico. Flute music sounded from the spacious courtyard, though only a handful of patrons could be seen exercising in the sun. The most exclusive club in Rhodos, the Diagoraseum was seldom crowded.

Amynias kept silent as they walked, and Lyceas grew anxious. He was possessed of a high-strung temperament and, although he had accepted Amynias as a friend and business partner, the man's scheming nature often made him uneasy.

"What news are you referring to?" he finally asked.

Amynias halted with a grim expression. "You remember my cousin, Korax? It seems he has come home."

Lyceas cringed, his belly tightening. "But how is that possible?"

Amynias resumed his walking. He spoke in quiet, strained tones. "I don't know. I just heard the news this morning, from one of my uncle's slaves. Korax arrived in Rhodos yesterday, on a ship from Egypt. He has money and a huge barbarian slave that he calls his bodyguard."

Lyceas stumbled along in dismay. For him, the events surrounding Korax's disappearance had been suppressed, but never forgotten. In fact, those events had been the beginning of his close association with Amynias. The plot to prevent Korax's return to Rhodes had forged a strange, unwholesome bond among the four young men who took part. Amynias alone seemed to have profited from that bond, using it to insinuate himself into a closer relationship with Lyceas, Patrollos, and their families. When the young men had completed their military service, Amynias accepted a post in the lending house owned by Lyceas' father. Within two years, he had become a partner. On reflection, one might almost say that instigating the plot to betray his cousin had launched all of Amynias' good fortune.

To Lyceas, in contrast, those events were a buried source of guilt and worry. At times they still haunted his nightmares.

And now the nightmares were coming true.

"What are you going to do?" he demanded.

Amynias shrugged. "I suppose I will send a note welcoming my cousin home, perhaps invite him to dinner once he has settled in. It would seem unnatural if I didn't."

"But aren't you worried that—"

"No. The attack was years ago, a foolish quarrel among boys. Best forgotten by all of us."

"I'm not only talking about that. The ransom!"

Amynias' stride did not falter. "There is no proof we were involved."

No proof? Struggling against a rising panic, Lyceas tested that idea against his memories ...

It had happened in the spring, during the Festival of Dionysus. A party and singing competition was held for the young cadets of Rhodes, in the Guild Hall of Aphrodite. Lyceas attended with Amynias, their friend Patrollos, and Cimon, Patrollos' cousin. All of them participated, composing and singing hymns to Aphrodite or Dionysus. But they had left the hall in disgrace after Korax sang clever rhymes to mock them. Humiliated, they had skulked about the town all night, drinking far too much, plotting revenge. The revenge had come at dawn. The four of them caught up with Korax in a narrow lane in the tradesmen's quarter. They only meant to beat him, but in his rage Patrollos lost control, dashing Korax's head against the cobblestones. They had fled in panic, leaving Korax for dead—only to learn the next day that, miraculously, he still lived.

Bound by guilt, the four young men waited in fear for Korax to accuse them. When no accusations came, Amynias suggested a more frightening possibility. It was known in the family, he said, that Korax's mother was a witch. Perhaps he *had* been dead, and his mother's witchcraft had brought him back. Perhaps she and Korax would make no public accusations, but instead plan a more horrible revenge.

Amynias insisted this idea was even more plausible when Korax, though not fully recovered, was put on a ship bound for Thrace—Thrace, the home of his mother's people, the land of witches. Just over a month later, Fate took another twist. Amynias reported that Korax's ship had been waylaid by pirates, that the young Rhodian was being held hostage. That was when Amynias suggested a despicable solution: find the pirate agent who would convey the ransom and pay him an extra sum—to ensure Korax would not return. Lyceas had been horrified by the idea, but too frightened to object. Patrollos and Cimon had railed against the dishonor, even calling Amynias a serpent. But in the end, they had all agreed. Lyceas still recalled their meeting with the pirate's courier, a greasy, disreputable rogue ...

"There is no proof we were involved," he muttered, "except for that pirate agent, Bolocrates."

"To whom we never gave our names," Amynias reminded him. "Even if that man was somehow discovered, and he remembered our faces well enough to identify us, who would believe his word over ours? The whole story would sound absurd."

They had reached the courtyard and now stopped beside one of the sand wresting circles. Amynias reached a hand onto his shoulder blade and arched his spine. Lyceas joined him in leaning and stretching.

But then another thought occurred. He moved close to Amynias' ear.

"You're forgetting something else. You convinced us all to betray Korax because we feared his sorcery. Now he has come back, and from Egypt. What if he has become a sorcerer indeed, and plans to revenge himself on us?"

Amynias glared, but gave no answer. Moments later, he stepped to the center of the circle. Reluctantly, Lyceas joined him to begin their bout. The two men braced their feet and laid hands on each other's shoulders.

Suddenly, Amynias murmured: "You are correct, we must watch him. At the first hint of sorcery, we must be prepared to rid ourselves of him—for certain this time."

They grappled, but Lyceas' sinews had gone slack. After a brief struggle, Amynias caught him with a hip-throw, and Lyceas landed hard on his rump.

"Brother, if I might have a word with you." Arms crossed over his broad chest, Zeno halted before his brother's couch.

Leontes blank stare never strayed from the brightness of the open balcony. "What is it?"

"I spent the morning with your son. We went over all of our current ventures and accounts. Korax is going to help me manage things. His brain is nimble and clever, as it always was. He is going to be a great help to us..."

Leontes' face showed a loss of interest.

"I want you to work with him," Zeno said. "To teach him what you remember."

The old man twitched as though bitten by a horsefly. "No. I can't, Zeno."

"Please, brother." Zeno sat down on the edge of the couch. "This side of the business is not my strength. I'm sure you know methods and shortcuts I never learned. And there is all your knowledge of our partners overseas. It would help us all if you would try."

"I remember almost nothing. Do not ask this of me."

Zeno's look hardened. "I ask it for another reason, a better reason. I want you to spend time with your son, to welcome him *as* your son."

Leontes moaned and covered his ears. "Leave me in peace."

"Do not be so stubborn!" Zeno grabbed his brother's wrists and yanked them down. "Your son who was lost to us has returned, after much hardship and grief. Instead of rejoicing, you've only added to his suffering."

"Do not talk to me of suffering! You still have your wife. You still have your house. You still have your eyes. All of that has been taken from me."

"You still have your son," Zeno said, rising stiffly. "A fine young man, returned to you like a gift from the gods. Take care that you do not lose him a second time."

Leontes glared from his sightless eyes. "Would you please leave me in peace? Or, if my presence in your house is too much of a burden, tell me so and I will go out into the streets and beg for my living."

Zeno shook his head mournfully. "There is no use in arguing with an old fool." He turned on his heels and trudged from the room.

The map was drawn on four sheets of papyrus pasted together. All the lands and waters visited by the family's ships were depicted, the coastlines and ports drawn in fine detail. Tiny figures carved of wax represented the vessels, in harbors or on the open sea.

Perched on a tall stool, Korax stared at the map and the ships, his eyes shifting from time to time, his body perfectly still. The broad table stood in the corner of his chamber, positioned near the balcony to take advantage of the daylight. Korax sat here for an hour or more each morning.

Guarding the good fortune of most of the ships was easy. The flow of events surrounding their voyages seemed already favorable. But in some cases malicious circumstances hovered along the way—ill-timing, problems with cargo, dead calms. In a few instances, dangers threatened—storms or encounters with pirates. In his mind, Korax wrestled against both the nuisances and the perils. He whispered charms over the waxen ships, envisioned them bathed in protective light.

Now his hand moved from his lap. His forefinger nudged one of the ships to a new position in the western sea. That ship, currently plying the Italian coast, seemed in particular danger. Spurred by worry, Korax had cast workings over it every morning. But something opposed his efforts, some huge, mysterious force, as if the great sea itself was determined to wreck the ship. Probing the force, Korax sensed a malevolent will of enormous strength— an unknown god.

"You sense correctly." Athene's voice came unbidden into his mind. "There is a god who opposes your work."

"Who is he?" Korax asked. "Is it possible to appease him?"

"Can you not recognize him? You have met before."

Korax gazed down at the endangered ship. At the back of his mind he perceived a dark face, a beast with a long, pointed snout.

"Set of the Egyptians." Korax shivered. "But why should he be concerned with the ships of Rhodes? Has he followed me here?"

"In a sense, he has. By opposing his priest in Memphis, you made him an enemy. But his realm is not restricted to Egypt. The Greeks know him by another name."

"Poseidon?" Korax whispered, for that name had entered his thoughts. "I am bewildered, goddess. Are you saying that Set and Poseidon are one?"

"In a way." Athene sounded almost amused. "We gods are not constrained to inhabit a single vessel, as mortals are. The images you have of us are images created by men. Our spirits flow from one form to another with ease. To the Egyptians, Set is Lord of the Abyss. To Greeks, Poseidon is god of the sea and maker of earthquakes. Both images embody the forces of strife and destruction. That is why, in your tales, Poseidon is sometimes my foe. For I am the preserver of cities."

"The nature of the gods is hard to comprehend," Korax grunted. "But putting that aside, how can I counter him?"

"A bold question! I like your nerve, Korax of Rhodes. But pitting your mortal will against his full power would be foolhardy.

Instead, you must tug and prod to bring your ships safely home. When you feel the opposing force to be overwhelming, then withdraw from the struggle. But come back the next day and start again. Little by little, even a god's will can be overcome."

Next morning, Korax's contemplation of the map was interrupted. At the far end of the chamber, the door creaked open. Deep in concentration, Korax had heard no knocking.

"Your pardon, master." Phoemio poked his head into the room. "I have brought your father to speak with you."

"Of course." Korax hopped from the stool.

Leontes shuffled in, leaning on Phoemio's arm. The old man looked haggard, but his beard had been clipped, his hair combed and oiled. Korax brought a chair. Phoemio helped the old master to sit, then discreetly withdrew.

"Are you there, Korax?"

"Yes father, right here."

"Zeno has been pressing me to work with you. I told him I don't think I can be of any help, but he keeps pestering me. Since he will give me no peace otherwise, I have agreed to try."

"I welcome your help," Korax replied. Awkwardly, he scanned his work table, looking for some business he could discuss with his father. He shifted some documents, found a thick pile of papyrus.

"Perhaps you can advise me on these letters. Zeno gave me all of his correspondences going back several years. I've read some of them, but I don't know the authors and don't understand many of the questions involved."

"Yes, very well," Leontes said.

Korax went through the letters one by one. His father offered a comment here and there, but it was obvious his heart was not in the work. Most of the documents came from trading partners overseas. In many cases, Leontes claimed not to remember the men or recognize their names.

But when Korax mentioned the letter from Boethus of Abdera in Thrace, Leontes raised his head with a pained expression.

"He is your mother's brother, you know?"

"Yes. He writes that my grandfather has died, and that he is now responsible for their business. He writes to Zeno, but he sends you his greetings and his hope that your health is improving."

Leontes' eyes moistened. "Your mother was such a wild, lovely girl. I should not have taken her from her home. Her life in Rhodes was never happy."

Korax set down the papyrus. "She loved you, father. And me."

"Yes, and look what it brought her! You were not here to see it, Korax, how she suffered at the end."

His heart unstrung, Korax knelt before his father's chair. "I know that you feel it is my fault, and that you have a right to feel that way. I am sorry for what I did."

Leontes' moan was loud and ragged. Clumsily, he patted Korax's wrist. "I don't blame you. It was Fate. We are all helpless before the whims of the gods."

"No, father. We make our own fates, at least to some degree. I am convinced."

"Oh." Leontes reflected. "Your mother believed that also. She was wise about such matters."

"Yes."

"She was gifted, too. She knew mysterious, wonderful things. I never learned about them. I was afraid to. But, I think she believed that you inherited her gifts."

"Perhaps I did."

Leontes gave a weak and fretful laugh. "Yes. Phoemio confides to me that you came back from Egypt a great magician, that you are going to save us all from ruin."

"Phoemio imagines much, and speaks far too much," Korax declared with irritation. He resolved to rebuke the slave for his loose tongue.

Leontes continued in a trembling voice: "I cannot deny that your mother used her arts to help the family's fortunes. But if that is your intention, you have a steep and stony path to climb. I cannot help anymore. I am too old and used up."

Korax rested a hand on the old man's frail shoulder. "It's all right, father. You can leave these troubles to me now."

Chapter Five

I still do not understand the purpose of this mission," Leukon complained as they marched down the hilly street. "You are carrying money from your uncle to pay your cousin for his house, but it is your uncle who owns the house."

"Yes," Korax replied patiently. "My uncle owns the house, but he borrowed money on it to help finance the family's shipping ventures. By lending him this money, my cousin Amynias acquired an interest in the house. This is called a loan. My uncle must pay back a little of the loan each month. The payment includes a portion of the original sum, plus an extra fee, which is my cousin's profit."

"But if your uncle needed this money and your cousin had it, why didn't your cousin simply give the necessary amount?"

"Because he is in the business of lending money," Korax answered. "And while he could have made it a gift, for the sake of family loyalty, he chose not to show such generosity."

Leukon stroked his chin, perturbed. "So your cousin takes advantage of his kinsman's misfortune for his own profit. Isn't this considered dishonorable?"

"That would depend on whom you asked. But since you are asking me, yes, I consider it dishonorable."

The Celt nodded, satisfied on the point. "So then, why did you volunteer to carry this money to your villainous cousin?"

"Well, to be frank, there is a history of bad blood between Amynias and myself. Since I will need to see him sooner or later, I choose to take him by surprise, to see him on my terms rather than his own."

"Hmm." Leukon clenched his lips unhappily. "And why are you involving me in this sordid business?"

"Because I want him to see you also. Together we'll make a stronger impression than I would make alone."

They approached the gate of Amynias' house. It was still early morning, and the sun cast long, cool shadows over the street. Korax rapped sharply on the varnished door. After a short time the small, suspicious gatekeeper appeared.

"I am here to see your master. Tell him his cousin Korax has brought the mortgage payment from Zeno."

The man led them in to the courtyard then scuttled off to convey the message. While Leukon waited solemnly by the gate, Korax looked around.

The house was much changed from what Korax remembered: new statues under the peristyle, gilded rails on the upper gallery, expensive rugs and tapestries visible in the interior rooms. At the far end of the courtyard, his mother's garden had been demolished, the space paved over with masonry.

"Cousin, so good of you to pay me this visit."

Amynias strolled from under the peristyle, a sea-green himation draped over his long chiton. He seemed taller than Korax remembered, wider in the shoulders. With his high forehead and haughty carriage, he looked very much the successful young banker. He evinced an air of friendliness and easy self-assurance, except when his eyes flicked warily over the tall Celt.

"My man, Leukon," Korax said, clasping his cousin's wrist. "He's quite tame, I assure you. He accompanies me everywhere. I'm educating him in our ways."

"I see. How novel," Amynias replied. "I trust you received my letter, and that you will accept my invitation to dine. I'm so anxious to hear all about your travels."

A spasm of rage flashed through Korax. It took all his self-control to keep his face neutral. "To be blunt, I think it best I decline your invitation."

Amynias looked disappointed. "Really? But why?"

When Korax merely looked at him, Amynias continued with a note of sadness. "I hope, cousin, you are not still harboring resentment about the past. Regrettable things occurred between us, but I think we were all to blame. We were young and rash. I had hoped we could put those incidents behind us and start anew as friends."

"I can forgive what was done by young men in anger." Korax spoke with deliberate inflection. "But there are other kinds of betrayal I cannot forgive."

He let his words settle in and observed their effect on Amynias—uncertainty, a rising alarm. Korax lifted the coin pouch in his hand.

"I have brought you Zeno's payment."

"Oh ... That is what you mean? You are angry with me because I charge our uncle interest? But Korax, surely you must see that's only business, nothing more."

Korax's voice retained its quiet edge. "What I see is you growing rich, while the rest of the family suffers. I see you reaping profits from the hardships of your two uncles, men who provided for you when you were a boy and your mother was widowed. These are not the deeds of a rash youth. And they are not the actions of a man I could call a friend." He handed Amynias the purse. "I require a written receipt."

Amynias scowled. "Zeno never asked for that before."

"We will from now on. It's only business, nothing more."

"Fair enough. Come to my office." Amynias pivoted and walked off, calling over his shoulder: "Oh, and you can leave your henchman here. You'll be quite safe, I assure you."

Korax gestured for Leukon to wait, then stalked after his cousin. They went to the room that used to be Leontes' study. Like the rest of the house, it contained extravagant new furnishings.

While Amynias counted the money, Korax's gaze wandered over the cluttered writing table. He noticed a high stack of documents that appeared to be cargo manifests and listings of ports of call. Naturally, a banker might study such information about ships he invested in. Still, it seemed a little odd that Amynias had collected so many.

As if sensing his curiosity, Amynias shifted the stack to another corner of the table. He dipped a stylus in an inkpot and scrawled a receipt on a fresh sheet. He rolled it up and presented it to Korax.

Korax unrolled the papyrus and read it thoroughly.

"I regret you are so unwilling to trust me or to regard me as your friend," Amynias said. "I have close relations with many important men now. I could be quite helpful to you."

Korax eyed him coolly. "I think it best we follow our separate paths."

As they walked back to the courtyard, Korax added: "I have one other question. Three years ago I sent several letters from Alexandria to my father and mother. I gave explicit instructions that they be delivered to this house. Neither Zeno nor my father ever saw any of them."

Amynias grunted derisively. "You accuse me of stealing letters now? What possible reason could I have for that?"

"I cannot imagine."

Amynias halted in his tracks and replied emphatically: "After I took possession of this house, Leontes received a number of correspondences. I forwarded them all to Zeno, I assure you."

He sounded appropriately offended by the suggestion that he might have acted improperly. But Korax noted an uneven slant to the shoulders, a hooded look in the eyes. He sensed his cousin was lying.

Korax dropped his gaze and answered blandly. "Very well, then. That is what I thought you would say."

Korax slashed his sword through the air, hacking savagely. The wood blade struck Leukon's shield with a force that shuddered in Korax's shoulder. Immediately he leaped back, avoiding the Celt's stabbing riposte.

They practiced on a tree-bordered lawn of the Heliochora, the public gymnasium. The sweat of their exertion dripped and sprayed from their naked bodies as they fought back and forth. They came here almost every afternoon. Training with sword and buckler had become Korax's favored form of exercise. The violent bouts offered a much-needed release for his pent up frustrations and worries.

As they fought, Korax glimpsed someone through the corner of his eye. A young man or boy, wrapped in a yellow himation, had taken a seat on a marble bench to watch their skirmish. The presence of the giant Celt in the field often attracted a curious audience, but something about this fellow Korax found distracting.

Leukon took advantage of his master's inattention. The round point of his wood sword poked hard into Korax's belly. Korax sailed off his feet, grunting with pain, and landed with a shudder on his backside.

"Hah, you dropped your guard, Blackbird," Leukon cried in unfettered triumph. "You must keep your mind on your fighting."

Korax clutched his stomach. "I think you've finished me for the day." He groaned as Leukon raised him to his feet. "Go and have your bath. I will meet you at the outer porch."

Humming merrily, the Celt gathered up the swords and bucklers and headed off toward the gymnasium's massive colonnade. Panting, Korax regarded the young man in yellow who sat watching. He was older than Korax had first thought, definitely a grown man and not a boy, though his long, curling hair and effeminate features were reminiscent of Dionysus.

The man smiled, and suddenly Korax knew him—Staphylus! They had been schoolmates together, close friends. Like Korax himself, Staphylus was a lover of poetry and song. In fact, they had been crowned co-champions on that fateful night five years past, Korax for his song to Aphrodite, Staphylus for a hymn to Dionysus.

Grinning, Korax walked over, stiff and slightly bent due to his bruised stomach. He extended his hand, but Staphylus jumped up and hugged him.

"I wondered how long it would take you to recognize me. I was so happy to hear that you had returned to Rhodos—happy and astonished."

"It has been a long time," Korax murmured, sitting down. "And I have been through many changes."

"You are looking fit." Staphylus appraised his nudity with appreciative eyes. "Though not so fit as your Celtic titan. What a gorgeous specimen he is!"

Korax nodded, taking a certain pride in the impressive Celt. "An intellectual man too, believe it or not. He is reading *The Iliad*."

"You don't mean it. Amazing! But tell me about yourself. Is it true you lived in Alexandria? I've always wanted to visit there."

"You would love it, my friend. The intellectual life is beyond compare. The Library alone you would find worth the journey— not to mention the endless performances."

"So I have often heard," Staphylus responded. "We have a modest Salon of the Muses here in Rhodos now. You must come and listen, whenever you are able. Though, to be honest, we lost our leading light over a year ago. Apollonius, the author of *The Voyage of the Argo*. Do you know it?"

"Oh, yes. I heard his premiere recitation in Alexandria. It was a triumph."

"How wonderful," Staphylus said. "I do miss Apollonius, such a talented and beautiful man."

Korax stood, the pain in his belly having subsided. "Walk with me to the baths," he suggested.

They strolled along a winding path, past bronzes and broad, leafy oaks. In the shade of one tree, a teacher was lecturing to a group of schoolboys.

"I met Apollonius once," Korax recalled. "He mentioned his love for Rhodos, but also how a pall had descended over the city. I must say, I've found that description accurate."

"Oh, I agree. It doesn't take the sensitivity of a great poet to notice it. The town is suffering. Commerce is half what it used to be."

"So I understand," Korax said. "My uncle blames bad weather, extended dead calms in the West."

"I've heard that also. But mostly it's the pirates. They've grown much stronger. You've heard about the battle last year off Karpathos? They fought our navy to a draw."

Korax knew of the disaster. One third of the Rhodian fleet had been lost in a single, bloody engagement. In theory, King Ptolemy's navy was supposed to police the Aegean. But Ptolemy's only concern seemed to be to keep Antigonus Gonatas landlocked. Egypt's powerful Aegean fleet seldom left its base at Andros, except to mount an occasional blockade against one of the Greek ports.

"Enough gloomy talk," Staphylus declared. They had reached the gymnasium courtyard, filled with wrestlers, idlers, and the tuneful voices of flutes. "You must come and dine with me, and you must agree to attend our salon. Do you still play the lyre?"

JACK MASSA

"Oh, sometimes. My relationship with the instrument has been sporadic over the years."

"That's a pity. I remember very clearly how well you played and sang."

They mounted stone steps and passed through the portico. Entering the huge, crowded bathing hall, Korax found his kit on a shelf along the wall. He dowsed himself with sand from a ceramic basin, took his strigil, and began to scrape off the sweat and grime.

Staphylus watched him fondly. "I'll never forget that competition at the Guild Hall of Aphrodite, when we both won first prize. It was just before you took ill and had to leave Rhodos. Do you remember Berenicea, the courtesan that you chose that night? She is a friend of mine now, one of the leading hetaeras of the city. She sometimes hosts our salon at her home."

"Really ...?" Mention of Berenicea brought Korax a stream of poignant recollections. Her blue eyes and red hair, her sweet and gentle manner. She was one of the first girls he bedded. That night, he had been certain he would love her forever.

"Forgive me, I did not mean to stir up painful memories."

"Nonsense." Korax scraped his arm deliberately. "It's nothing."

"Well, I'm not usually such a gossip. But since I brought it up, I must mention one other thing. Berenicea has a short, exclusive list of clients. One of them is Patrollos. I know you remember him."

"Oh, yes." Korax paused, remembering now the aftermath of that night—Patrollos choking him, smashing his head on the street. "And you say Berenicea is his lover?"

"I hope I have not upset you."

Korax resumed his vigorous strigiling. "Not in the least. I am steering clear of Patrollos and his crowd, and I am also steering clear of the entanglements of love. At this phase in my life, I have concluded that is best."

"I see." Staphylus seemed a shade dubious. "Well then, there's no reason you can't attend our salon."

"None in the least."

"I am glad. And you must dine with me as well. I will send an invitation. You are staying at your uncle's house, correct?"

"Yes. But you've not told me about yourself, Staphylus. Are you still living with your parents? Is poetry your only occupation?"

"Oh, I wish it was. No, my father would never approve of my spending all my time on such idleness. To please him, I've taken up study of the law. He is a magistrate now, and I assist at his office. Also I take on clients of my own. Should you ever need a legal advisor ... Well, for my friends, my fees are very low."

He finished with a muted laugh, but Korax nodded in all seriousness.

"I will certainly remember that. I don't know what troubles may be coming my way, but all my instincts tell me there will be some."

Chapter Six

The smallest of Rhodos' three harbors was the military port. It lay north of the city, separated from the main harbor by a long, fortified mole. Around its broad quays were the naval shipyards, with their enclosed boathouses, carpentry shops, barracks, and armories—all guarded by Rhodian marines.

In the late afternoon, a few days before the midsummer Festival of Helios, Amynias and Lyceas waited on the docks among a crowd of civilians. They watched as a squadron of warships advanced across the blue harbor. The galleys came on with beating oars, five quadriremes, four of the smaller triremes, and the proud flagship, a massive quinquereme that carried five oarsmen at every thwart.

The beat of the time-keepers' drums drifted faintly over the water. The crews had lowered sails and stowed their masts. The ships needed no dockhands with hawsers and boathooks to guide them into their slips. Instead, to the cheers of the spectators, each vessel turned smartly, the oarsmen backing water. With expert handling, the galleys sidled neatly to rest against the docks.

Amynias applauded politely as each vessel touched its mooring, but he did not join in the hurrahs of the crowd. The masterful display of seamanship only reminded him of his own days at the oars, days he recalled with distaste. The navy had never suited him—backbreaking drudgery, pompous officers, far too many regulations.

Besides, he had other problems on his mind today.

With Lyceas at his side, he strode along the dock toward the quinquereme. The imposing galley stood over one-hundred feet long, with high fighting platforms at stern and prow. She was newly-commissioned, one of the first of the larger class warships built by the Rhodians in response to the disaster at Karpathos. Amynias himself had helped arrange the financing.

Trumpets sounded as the crews assembled on the decks. Amynias waited while the ships companies were reviewed by their officers, then finally dismissed. Sailors, rowers, and armored marines swarmed down the landing planks, to a new round of cheering from the crowd. Many of the men were met by the embraces of family members or the eager kisses of wives. Amynias watched from the background until spotting two tall officers in corselets and cloaks, among the last to leave the quinquereme. He and Lyceas marched forward to intercept them.

"Patrollos and Cimon, welcome home, noble men of Rhodes."

Cimon responded with a quick, uneasy smile. But Patrollos glowered under the visor of his crested helmet. Patrollos often seemed unhappy to meet him, Amynias reflected. That would be especially true today.

"What brings you to the navy port?" Patrollos inquired warily as they clasped forearms.

"We heard you had shore leave for the Festival. We ... uh, have some news," Lyceas explained lamely.

His nervousness, of course, made Patrollos and Cimon all the more puzzled and suspicious.

Amynias was conscious of the other people milling on the dock. "I thought you might show us the ship," he suggested. "After all, our bank raised much of the capital. We'd like a look at the splendid craft we helped to purchase for Rhodes."

Cimon grunted as though the idea was idiotic, but Patrollos grasped the meaning.

"Of course," he said, thin-lipped. "We'd be glad to give you the tour."

He turned with a sweep of his cloak and led them up the gangplank. They stepped onto the long middle-deck, deserted now except for a few sailors stowing gear and lashing down lines. The quinquereme carried six ballistas, huge cross-bows with a deadly range twice that of human archers. But her most impressive feature was the turrets, tall fighting platforms erected at stern and bow.

Wordlessly, Patrollos marched across the deck and ascended the ladder of the forward turret. Amynias went after him, then Lyceas and Cimon. They climbed onto a square platform, high above the foredeck. From here they could see over the city walls, down into the streets of Rhodos. The sun was sinking in the west among crimson clouds. To the east, the giant Helios stood against a dim sky, his back toward them.

"Now we are alone," Patrollos said. "What is the real reason you are here?"

"It is Korax," Lyceas blurted. "He has returned to Rhodos."

Amynias observed their reactions. Cimon went white and rigid. Patrollos shut his eyes in grim resignation, as though he had already guessed.

The four of them had shared the secret for more than five years—that they had assaulted Korax and left him for dead, then later paid the pirate's agent to arrange for his disappearance. Now they eyed each other on the windy turret, each aware of how the conspiracy had affected them, coiling the strands of their lives together. Amynias wondered stolidly what this new twist of their combined fates would bring.

"Do we know what happened to him?" Patrollos asked.

"More or less," Amynias said. "The brigands shipped him off to the block. He was a slave in Egypt, then somehow gained his freedom and lived for a time in Alexandria. He returned just over a month ago, with a rather small fortune and a rather large bodyguard. Now he's living with his father and uncle, helping with their business."

"What are his intentions?" Cimon demanded. "Toward us, I mean."

"That is very hard to say. He stopped in to see me one morning. He claimed he was willing to forgive the attack."

"But you don't trust him," Patrollos surmised.

Amynias shook his head. "He tried to provoke me, hinted that he might know more than he was letting on."

"But he hasn't accused us of anything," Lyceas pointed out hopefully. "And he has had ample time."

"I told you he would never seek legal redress," Amynias replied with a note of scorn. "That is not his way."

"What are you suggesting?" Cimon growled. "Speak plainly for once!"

"My friend, I suggest first of all that you get hold of your nerves," Amynias answered placidly. "I am only saying it is too early to know what my cousin intends. My source inside my uncle's house reports certain statements, certain activities that might indicate Korax is practicing magic. Whether he plans to use sorcery to attack us—Well, so far there is no evidence."

Amynias experienced a tingle of perverse enjoyment as he observed their reactions. Cimon and Lyceas stood aghast, filled with horrible imaginings. Patrollos stared at him with loathing.

"I swear by my fathers, Amynias, I should never have allowed you to involve me in this base treachery."

Amynias pretended hurt feelings. "Really, Patrollos, it's unfair to blame me. You are the one who flew into a rage and spilled my cousin's brains out on the pavement. All along, I've only tried to shield you from the consequences."

"What do you think we should do?" Lyceas asked.

Amynias noted with satisfaction how they deferred to him now. Without even trying, he had taken leadership of the group away from the feckless Patrollos.

"For the present, watch and be on our guard. And, if Korax makes any move against us, be ready to strike back with decisive force. At least, that is my intention." He glanced over their tense faces and smiled. "Beyond that, I think Patrollos and Cimon should enjoy their shore leave, and we should all endeavor to enjoy the festival that lies ahead."

Patrollos lay on his belly in the warm bed, sniffing the scent of fresh linen and the lingering perfume of his mistress. Something smooth but insistent tickled the bare skin on his foot. He rolled over with a moan and buried his head under a pillow. Faintly, he heard Berenicea's laughter.

Suddenly the bed shook as she jumped astride his hips and yanked away the pillow. "Patrollos, my darling. The sun is halfway to its noon. You really must get up now."

He blinked reluctantly. He was sure he had drunk too much and as soon as he rose he would feel a terrible headache.

"What day is it?"

"The first day of the Festival of Helios. If you don't hurry you will miss the ceremony."

"I don't care."

"Oh. Come, my brave Achilles." Berenicea pulled his arm to make him sit up. "Your family expects you, and I have a banquet to prepare."

"Very well. Very well." Patrollos didn't like hearing mention of her other clients. He leaned elbows on his knees and massaged his scalp. As expected, his head pounded abominably.

"I tried to warn you. Unmixed wine is very bad for the liver." Berenicea handed him his gray chiton.

She was already dressed, had probably been up for hours. Her knee-length gown of green silk was cinched by a wide silver girdle. Her hair, the color of bright embers, was piled high on her head.

"Get dressed, my dear. You'll feel better when you've had your bath."

Patrollos eyed his garment dully. "No, I won't. I'm sure of it."

"Oh." Berenicea crawled onto the bed and hugged him, holding his face against her bosom. "What is troubling my poor Achilles? I've never seen you so miserable."

"I cannot tell you."

She leaned back, her red lips parted. "You can tell me anything, Patrollos. You know that."

His chin dropped. Perhaps he should tell her. It was only in her arms that he found any comfort or solace. He felt his shoulders heave and had to stop himself from crying.

"Tell me, my brave Achilles," she whispered, stroking the hair at the back of his neck.

"It concerns a man you might remember, Korax."

"Korax?"

"Yes." He decided to confess a part of it. Maybe that would ease the guilt a little. "Years ago, he shamed me at a singing competition, at the Hall of Aphrodite."

"Yes, I remember."

"Of course. You were the prize we both wanted so badly. But I never told you what happened the next day. I and some others waited for him. We had been drinking all night, and I ... lost my temper. I only meant to punish him for humiliating us, but I ended up beating him severely—nearly to death. After that, he was sent away from Rhodes, and ... it was rumored he was waylaid by pirates. No one knew for sure what happened. But now he has returned."

She searched his eyes, puzzled. "Why is that so terrible?"

"He says he does not seek revenge against us. But my friends are not so sure."

Her puzzlement deepened. "Even if that were so, I cannot believe you fear him."

"Of course not. I fear no danger to myself." That part was true. All of Amynias' scare-mongering about sorcery held no terror for Patrollos. What worried him was far worse. "If the tale of my crime were made public, it would dishonor me, disgrace my family. We—we left him on the street to die."

Briefly, her teeth showed in a grimace of repugnance at this shameful confession. But then her merciful heart reasserted itself, and she hugged him to her chest. "My poor Achilles. You carry such a burden. Your name and honor, they are so much for you to live up to. But if Korax didn't accuse you at the time, it is unlikely he would do so now. Have you spoken with him?"

"No."

"Well, then you must. Perhaps you worry over nothing. I think you must go to Korax, tell him you regret the attack. After all, it was the deed of a drunken youth. I do not think he would hold a grudge after all this time. But even if he does, you could offer to make amends, to pay him redress. He would surely accept that, if he is a man of honor."

Patrollos glanced into her wide, compassionate eyes. Quickly, he looked away. He could not hold her gaze and still conceal the rest of the truth—the more odious dishonor.

"Perhaps you are right. I should try to see him."

"Of course." She cradled him in her arms. After a moment, she had an inspiration. "I know how I can help you! I recall Korax to be a lover of poetry. The Salon of the Muses will convene here on the last night of the festival. I shall invite you and Korax. You can also bring your friends, the others who were involved in the trouble. Within my house, you will all be under the aegis of

Aphrodite. I will pray that she inspire your hearts with the spirit of reconciliation and forgiveness."

Chapter Seven

A t noon, the people of Rhodos filled the Square of the Colossus in front of the Temple of Helios. A sprawling crowd of citizens, foreigners, and slaves had gathered in festival finery. Many carried sun-staffs or ceremonial spears. Heads were crowned with wreathes of laurel, palm, or heliotrope. Despite the huge crowd, the square stood quiet, the only sound the measured, stately pounding of kettledrums.

At the center of the square, at the feet of the Colossus, lay a wide reflecting pool. Before the pool an altar had been erected, a giant slab of white marble. Hands raised in supplication, the priests of Helios offered up their prayers for the people. Near them stood the archons, admirals, and chief officials of the town. Members of all the ruling families watched in ranks behind them, draped in ceremonial robes of orange, yellow, and gold. Beside the altar, twelve prize rams were held on tethers, ready for the sacrifice. Their snowy fleeces were unblemished, and the gilding on their curved horns sparkled in the sunlight.

Korax watched from the colonnade of a stoa, at the far end of the plaza. Zeno, Callipatria, and the others of his family had gone down into the square to stand somewhere close to the Colossus. While the family's dwindled fortunes did not allow them to sponsor sacrifices or choral groups—which would have earned them the right to wear ceremonial robes and stand by the altar— they still wished to approach as close as they could to the city's god.

Korax had chosen not to go so near. As the ceremony proceeded, he let his restless eyes wander over the enormous musculature of the Colossus, to the proud head with its crown of spiking sunbeams.

He knew its story well, of course: It lived in his memory as vividly as any hero tale. It had begun a generation ago, during the Wars of the Successors when Alexander's generals and their heirs battled over the vast empire. Situated at the crossing of the main sea lanes between East and West, with its wealth of ships and excellent harbors, Rhodes was a prize that all of the rivals coveted. The Rhodians sought to preserve their independence by forging an alliance with Ptolemy, the ruler of Egypt. In reprisal Demetrius, son of the King of Macedonia, invaded the island with an army of 40,000 troops. Demetrius had earned the epithet Polycrates, "the Breaker of Cities." He laid siege to Rhodos with mobile towers and huge catapults. But the greatly outnumbered Rhodians defended their city with ingenuity and courage. Their redoubtable navy kept the harbors open and harried Demetrius' supply ships. Their citizens manned the walls with spear, bow, and sling—Korax's father and uncles fought among them. After a year of stalemate, Demetrius was forced to withdraw. In his haste, he left behind the towers and catapults. Opportunistically, the Rhodians sold the abandoned siege engines to Demetrius' enemy, Ptolemy. They used the money from the sale to commission an offering of thanks to their patron god. Within twenty years, the Colossus had been raised, a gigantic figure of Helios gazing east across the sea—the spear of the sun in one hand, the torch of freedom held high in the other. On its base the Rhodians placed this inscription:

> "To you, O Sun, the people of Dorian Rhodes set up this bronze statue reaching to Olympus, when they had calmed the waves of war and crowned their city with spoils. Not only over the seas, but also on land did they light the beautiful torch of unfettered freedom."

Pondering this history, Korax stared up into the god's face— strong, serene, majestic. Searching in his soul, he felt the echoing presence of Helios. Because of the magical rites he had enacted in

Alexandria, the spirit of the god still lived in his being, knitted into the fibers of sinew and nerve. By comparison, the divine presence in the ceremony before him seemed a faint reflection, a shadow. Korax still honored the rite of course, and he watched in mute attention as the prayers were offered and hymns sung. But, somehow, his very intimacy with Helios denied him the ability to worship with the community.

On returning to Rhodes, Korax had hoped to fully bind himself to his family and his city. Now he wondered if that were possible. He considered with a pang of regret that the practice of magic had set him apart from the Rhodians, just as it had his mother.

Down in the square, close to the Colossus, Patrollos stood with the other members of his family. In contrast to the bright orange and yellow of his robe, his face had a pale, sickish hue. As each ram was killed, the ritual screams of the women in the crowd raised his dull headache to a splitting pain.

Patrollos had arrived late at the temple and scarcely had time to don the ceremonial garb. His tardiness elicited a theatrical harangue from his excitable mother, Choronice. His father, Halitherses, expressed his stern displeasure more eloquently and painfully to Patrollos with a grim shake of his head.

Now the family was lined up together in their brilliant robes: Halitherses, tall and aristocratic, the lord of the House of Philophron; Choronice, nearly as tall, a slim woman with elegant, high-set cheekbones; Patrollos himself, the eldest son; and next to him his little sister, Thalia. Only his brother Agesilaus was missing. Two years younger than Patrollos, Agesilaus was a junior officer on a quadrireme, patrolling somewhere in the eastern seas.

The throat of another ram was slit and Patrollos winced as the females let loose their high-pitched shrieks. After screaming with the rest, Thalia patted his arm consolingly. Turning to her, Patrollos saw a knowing smile that blended sympathy and amusement at his distress.

Patrollos sighed. His sister was a lovely girl with narrow, cunning eyes and her mother's excellent cheekbones. Though short by the family's standards, she had a neat figure and proud bearing. She also had that desirable rarity among Grecian women, naturally golden hair. Today, she had embellished her beauty with a necklace of amber beads and yellow sunbursts painted on her cheeks.

Like everyone in the family, Patrollos had a soft heart for little Thalia. That was her problem, of course. Since childhood, she had been spoiled excessively. Her parents had reaped the unhappy consequences after the willful girl reached marriageable age. Patrollos comforted himself with the thought that Thalia's scandalous behavior made his own infractions seem insignificant by comparison.

At least, those infractions his parents knew about.

Patrollos sighed once again, more woefully. Perhaps Berenicea was right. Meeting with Korax at a social occasion might prove that he meant them no harm after all. At least it would give Patrollos a chance to face the enemy and look him in the eye.

The guilt of what he had done to Korax was like a disease in Patrollos. At times it faded into remission, but it always returned to sicken and weaken him. A thousand times he wished he had owned up to his deed at the time, instead of letting Amynias talk him into his vile plot.

How he had come to loathe Amynias. The man was a snake. He had used the guilt of the other young men as an opening to wind himself into their confidence and win the friendship of their families. Patrollos had watched with repugnance as Amynias turned their shameful crime to his advantage.

And now Amynias had gotten his coils around little Thalia.

The last of the ram carcasses was carried off to be butchered. The hollow song of an aulos swelled in the air, and the priests sang a hymn of praise to the Sun. The hindquarters of the twelve rams, wrapped in fat and incense, were burned on the wide altar. As the smoke rose, more fires were lit in brick pits around the square. The flesh of rams and ewes was boiled in cauldrons and roasted on spits, enough for the entire town to share. While the ritual meal was cooked, the first of the choral groups gathered in front of the Colossus and began their performance.

The priests of Helios and the leading families filed across the square and mounted the steps of the grand temple. Inside the cool, high colonnade, scores of dining couches had been arranged. Here the elite of Rhodes could gaze down on the crowd and the performances and take their share of the sacred meal in comfort.

Patrollos and his family settled on couches near the temple's main doors, not far from the receiving line where the high priests and archons welcomed the distinguished citizens. Patrollos noticed Lyceas and his father, Theadetus the banker, and gave them both a curt nod as they ambled by in the milling crowd. He seized a cup from the tray of a passing servant and gratefully gulped down the chilled wine.

He had just emptied the cup when he saw with chagrin Amynias striding towards their place. Behind him came his mother Epiteleia, bustling to keep up with her son's brisk pace. She was dressed in the most garish gold costume imaginable and had dyed her hair a flaming orange.

Amynias, in a simple and neatly draped yellow robe, walked up boldly to Patrollos' parents. "Happy feast day to you, honored Halitherses and Choronice. Greetings, Patrollos and Thalia. Great is Helios in his blessings to Rhodes!"

Halitherses stood and clasped his hand. "Welcome, Amynias and Epiteleia. You will join our party, of course."

"Oh, thank you, yes," Epiteleia gushed. "We would be most splendidly gratified."

Patrollos spied a flicker of dismay at the corner of his mother's smiling mouth. Choronice could not abide the vulgar Epiteleia.

"But we are short one couch," remarked Thalia, the only one of the family who had not risen.

As she noted, there was only one empty couch in the group arranged around their central table.

"No bother," Epiteleia declared. "Amynias and I can share. The Goddess knows we've done it often enough over the years."

"Nonsense." Halitherses took charge. "You sit there, dear lady. Amynias can have Patrollos' place next to Thalia. Patrollos, go and tell the attendants to bring another couch."

Suppressing a pang of resentment, Patrollos bowed and walked off to comply. He ignored the cordial word of thanks that Amynias tossed at his back.

It was all Thalia's fault that the family had to grovel like this to Amynias. Two years ago, Thalia had been betrothed to a wealthy merchant, a middle-aged man from one of the ruling families. But Thalia had never been pleased with the match arranged by her father, and as the wedding approached she announced she was breaking it off. She had fallen in love with a professional charioteer, the son of a wheelwright. Despite importunities and threats from her father, and lavishly histrionic scenes by her mother, Thalia remained adamant: she would marry her dashing chariot racer and none other. If her parents refused, she vowed to run off with the man. Finally, Halitherses relented. He negotiated a settlement with the merchant that salvaged half of the dowry, then gave his daughter to the husband of her choice.

The marriage lasted six months. Thalia returned repeatedly to her parents' house, claiming tearfully that her husband was a brute, that he had never loved her. Finally, she appeared with bruises and a cut lip and vowed never to set foot in his house again. The chariot driver lodged a counter-complaint, swearing he had discovered his young wife in the embrace of one of his friends, another charioteer. To minimize the scandal, Halitherses negotiated a speedy divorce. The husband, of course, kept the dowry.

Now, nearly twenty, Thalia was back in her parent's house: no longer a virgin, with a ruined marriage and accusations of adultery attached to her, and one-and-a-half rich dowries already spent. The prospects of her finding a suitable husband seemed flimsy indeed, and then Amynias appeared on the scene. He claimed to be attracted solely by Thalia's beauty and charm, though it was plain that marrying into a ruling family was also a prime consideration. Still, he was a man of respectable family and rising wealth, and he offered to take the girl with only a token dowry. For these reasons, Halitherses viewed him as a most desirable son-in-law and was anxious to fix the match.

For her part, Thalia was not opposed, for she obviously found Amynias attractive. Still, perhaps to her credit, she insisted on a period of courtship, to allow the couple to know each other better.

"After all, father," she had said, "I would not wish to embarrass the family by acting imprudently again."

So now, as Amynias courted Thalia, the rest of the family was forced to court Amynias, for Halitherses was exceedingly anxious that the young banker not change his mind.

Reflecting on this despicable state of affairs, Patrollos returned with two temple attendants carrying an extra couch. He took his place opposite his parents.

The priests of Helios poured libations, and the savory roasted meat was served. The banquet commenced with a cheerful babble of conversation filling the portico. Below, on the temple steps, a chorus performed with flutes and dancing.

But the party around Halitherses' table was dominated by the voluble Epiteleia. Amynias' mother chattered incessantly, about the weather, the performances, the robes and shawls, the taste of the meat, and the fragrance of the wine. She compared all these items, in detail, to the like conditions and customs in her native Caria, a country that lay on the mainland north of Rhodes. All the while, Halitherses and Choronice listened politely, bleak smiles carved on their faces.

Meantime, Amynias conversed in secretive tones with Thalia, leaning in her direction and eliciting smirks and giggles.

Patrollos attempted to drown his misery in wine, but it only made his headache worse. Finally, when everyone had eaten, he suggested to Amynias that they take a stroll.

"I have an invitation to discuss with you," he said. "We can collect Lyceas and Cimon too."

Mention of those two men immediately conveyed to Amynias something about the topic of the proposed conversation. He showed a fleeting frown of puzzlement, but readily agreed. The two excused themselves and headed off. They stopped at the tables where Lyceas and Cimon sat and soon extricated them from their families.

The four men turned a corner of the colonnade and walked along the side of the grand temple. They stopped after passing nine tall pillars, well away from the babble of the feast and the crowds in the square.

"What is troubling you, Patrollos?" Amynias demanded.

"It's not trouble. As I said, I have an invitation, for the four of us. The Salon of the Muses is meeting two nights hence, at Berenicea's house."

"Sounds pleasant," Amynias answered. "But why the sudden interest in poetry? And why us four?"

"Berenicea's suggestion. She is also inviting Korax."

"What? Korax?" Lyceas muttered. He and Cimon exchanged fretful looks.

"It's an opportunity," Patrollos told them. "To meet him in a friendly gathering. I think it's a good idea."

Everyone looked at Amynias. His eyes shifted over their faces.

"I'm not sure what I think," he confessed. "What would be your purpose in confronting Korax?"

"I told you," Patrollos said, "to meet him in a friendly gathering. It would give us a chance to sound him out, to find out his intentions."

Amynias simpered. "Do you dream you are so perceptive as to read Korax's intentions? Believe me, you will see only what he wants you to see, and that can be treacherous."

"I will feel better if I look him in the eye," Patrollos answered. "And express my regret for assaulting him. That is the honorable thing. But it's only an invitation, Amynias. No one is forcing you to attend."

The four of them argued furtively back and forth, expressing doubts and suspicions, dissecting the simple party invitation as though it were a battle plan. Patrollos stared off in disgust, facing the hill of the city. From here, he could see the tradesman's warren, and beyond it the public stair where he had attacked Korax those long years ago.

"I have a question: Who is this Korax who has you all so unnerved?"

They whirled around to find Thalia, confronting them with an arch expression.

"Sister!" Patrollos admonished her. "I would hope at your age you'd show better manners than to eavesdrop."

Her mouth turned down. "Forgive me, brother. But if you are all so loutish as to keep your backs turned when a lady approaches, what am I supposed to do? I was sent by my mother and Epiteleia. They both are growing curious as to why you've been gone so long."

"We're returning now." Patrollos glanced furiously at Amynias. "I plan to attend the salon. The rest of you can do as you please."

Chapter Eight

The final day of the midsummer festival was dedicated to Tyche, Goddess of Fortune, as well as to Helios. Priests read divinations in the temples, and soothsayers told fortunes in the marketplace. People feasted at tables decked with garlands and cruised the harbor in pleasure boats.

Korax attended an afternoon banquet at Zeno's house. The upstairs dining room was crowded with family as in the old days. Callipatria hurried about, assisting the overworked slaves and thoroughly enjoying the festivities. Zeno's daughter Phaenna was visiting from the country, along with her husband Leochares and their children. Those children had been mere babes when Korax left Rhodos. Now little Carya, at thirteen, was changing into a young woman, while her brothers Autolycus and Damagetus were stout, robust boys of seven and nine. The children had not seen Korax since his return, and they pressed him for tales of his travels or to bring out his lyre and sing as he used to. But Korax had not touched the lyre since returning to Rhodes, and he pleaded that the stories would have to wait for another time.

Instead he talked business with his father and uncle and his cousin Isochomachus, whose presence at the banquet was unexpected. Zeno's son should have been in Ephesus by now. Two days from Rhodes, the ship he captained had been seized by pirates and stripped of her cargo, forcing his abrupt return.

"The seas are infested with brigands," he grumbled, "like termites in a rotten log."

"It's true," Zeno confirmed in his raspy voice. "They grow more numerous and brazen every year."

"Worse than that, they grow more efficient," Isochomachus said. "In the past when they snared a ship they'd take a few bales or jars. Now they seize whole cargos. They've developed networks of smugglers' ports and disreputable merchants," he explained to Korax. "It allows them to market whatever they steal. I swear by Poseidon, unless we find a way to scuttle them, it will be the end of honest trading. All of us will be forced to run as pirates."

"These things occur in cycles," Leontes remarked. "Zeno and I saw it also in our youth. The only cure is to build up our fleet till it is strong enough to sweep the brigands from the sea."

Korax was pleased that his father attended the banquet. The old man was taking more of an interest in things, helping Korax with letters and contracts, walking around the garden on Phoemio's arm. He even seemed to be seeing a little better.

"That's easier said than done, I'm afraid," Isochomachus answered gloomily. "Their hemiolias are swift and their captains cunning. Our galleys chase them from one stretch of the sea, and they just reappear somewhere else."

After dinner, the conversation continued outside on the terrace. Rather than drinking more wine and indulging in music or stories, the four men discussed the progress of the trading season and pored over ships' logs and ledgers.

"Our records are in much better shape now, thanks to Korax," Zeno declared. "I thank Zeus, who sent my dear nephew back to Rhodos to help us."

Korax appreciated the sentiment. He only wished he felt more successful. Since he had begun working with the map and the wax ships, three cargos had arrived safely in Rhodos. But the ships in the west seemed in constant danger, and Korax had completely missed the threat of the pirates who waylaid Isochomachus within a few leagues of the Rhodian coast.

Toward sunset, they were still rehearsing business matters when Phoemio appeared, leading a surprise visitor.

"Please forgive the intrusion." Staphylus stepped onto the terrace, wearing a laurel crown and carrying his lyre in a brocade bag. "I only need a brief word with Korax."

"It is no intrusion at all, young Staphylus." Zeno stood to clasp his hand. "I know your father, Agesandros the magistrate, a just and honorable man. Phoemio, a cup of wine for our guest."

For a short while, Staphylus sipped from a shallow cup and chatted politely with the party. But he took the first opportunity to draw Korax aside.

"What brings you here?" Korax asked, leaning on the terrace rail. "I thought we were to meet at Berenicea's house."

"We were. But I thought I'd better warn you. I went to her house this morning to go over the recital arrangements, and she showed me the guest list. It includes some old acquaintances of yours, Patrollos and Amynias chief among them."

"I see." Korax was taken aback. "I wondered about her motives when I received the invitation."

"Oh, her motives are virtuous. As these men have not attended the salon before, I asked her about them. She confessed that she wanted to bring you and Patrollos together under her roof, to give him a chance to make peace with you."

Korax considered. While he believed Amynias had plotted treachery against him, he was unsure to what extent Patrollos and the others were involved. If their guilt ran no deeper than the original attack, he ought to be willing to forgive that. Perhaps he could make peace with Patrollos.

"I don't know the details of your feud," Staphylus uttered quietly. "But I thought it only fair to warn you, in case you might want to change your mind about attending."

"Of course not." Korax straightened. "I'm not afraid of facing them. And I'm looking forward to the recital."

Staphylus brightened. "That's the fearless Korax I know and love. I'm heading there now. If you'd like to come with me, you could arrive before the other guests."

"That's not necessary. I will come later, as arranged."

Staphylus took his leave, and Korax resumed his conversation with Zeno and Isochomachus. Leontes had already retired, his meager reserves of energy drained by the excitement of the banquet and visitors.

Soon twilight came on, and Korax excused himself. Repairing to his chamber, he put on a fresh chiton and a leather headband with a lapis stone that he had purchased in Alexandria. He considered taking his lyre, which lay in its bag inside one of his chests, but decided against it. He had not played the instrument in months, and tonight he was definitely not in the mood for performing.

After putting on his sword belt and fastening a chlamys at his shoulder, he descended the house's grand staircase and crossed the courtyard. Before the gate, he was confronted by Phoemio, nervously wringing his hands. Beside him stood Leukon, arms crossed over his giant chest, long sword at his hip.

"And what do you two suppose you're doing?" Korax demanded.

"Your pardon, master," Phoemio began. "Master Staphylus disclosed his concerns to me. I know these are the same enemies who nearly killed you five years ago. Leukon and I are convinced you should not go tonight—at least not alone."

Korax chuckled with amazement. As always, Phoemio showed a knack for sponging up information. "I appreciate your concern, but this is silly. I am going to a poetry recital, not a war."

"It was also poetry last time," Phoemio reminded him. "The next morning, your poor mother and I had to scrape you off the street."

"Well, that was different. I won't be singing tonight." Korax spoke without irony, then laughed when he heard how the statement sounded like jest.

Phoemio and Leukon both failed to see the humor.

"You must take me along, Blackbird," the Celt announced firmly. "My instincts tell me you are in danger."

"I am sorry, but you were not invited," Korax replied. "Now kindly step out of my way."

But Leukon only stretched his spine, making himself even taller. "Why did you bring me to Rhodes if not to protect you? Five months in your service and I've been in one fight! Practicing with wooden swords is useless. I am losing all my skills and readiness!"

In fact, with the strenuous daily exercise at the gymnasium, the Celt looked fitter than ever. Still, Korax had noticed lately that Leukon seemed more morose and gloomy than usual. Obviously, the man was frustrated by boredom.

"If you have no real service for me," Leukon continued furiously, "then release me from my oath early and set me free."

"You are in no position to make demands of me," Korax answered, provoked by the Celt's display of rage. "I am your master. Both of you are my slaves, not my grandmothers. Kindly remember that, and kindly step out of my way."

He pushed past them roughly, opened the gate for himself and marched out into the darkening street.

Berenicea's house was built in a new neighborhood, high on the hill of Rhodos, near the theater. It was a villa in the Alexandrian style, similar to Zeno's mansion in architecture, though not so large. The walls were of rose-hued masonry, with carved entablatures and long, graceful balconies looking down on the street from the upper story.

The last twilight was fading as Korax approached the gate. From the balcony above came the music of lyres mingled with intermittent laughter. When he first received the invitation, Korax had experienced a pleasant, sentimental anticipation at the prospect of seeing Berenicea again. Now those feelings had evaporated in the tension of confronting Patrollos and his comrades.

A burly gatekeeper greeted him and checked his name against the guest list. The man ushered Korax into the courtyard, where he was met by a shapely courtesan. The woman conducted him to a tiled anteroom. She relieved him of his chlamys and sword, removed his sandals and washed his feet. She gave him a pair of soft, felt slippers, then led him by the hand up the central staircase.

Korax entered a bright banquet room with murals of sensual love scenes on the walls. Two sides of the chamber opened onto terraces, one overlooking the street, the other an inner courtyard. A score of dining couches were arranged along the sides of the room, most of them already filled.

Scanning the faces, Korax spotted Amynias and beside him a muscular, handsome man he knew at once was Patrollos. With them were two more. He recognized Cimon after a moment, and thought the other must be Lyceas. The men regarded him with wary, unsteady glances—all except Amynias, who nodded with the aloof visage of a statue.

Korax's eyes shifted and he recognized Berenicea. She had sat up when he entered and watched him with a slight, expectant smile. Her gown was dark green and her jewelry burnished copper, both complimenting the unmistakable red tresses piled atop her head. She looked as poised and regal as a queen.

"Welcome, my friend. Welcome." Staphylus stepped up and took Korax's arm.

Leading him across the mosaic floor, Staphylus introduced him to several friends, poets and patrons of the arts. A couple of them Korax remembered from former days, and they chatted pleasantly for a while. Then Staphylus brought him over to greet Berenicea. She rose and extended her hand. Korax bowed and kissed it.

"You are most welcome, my friend," she said. "I hope you will visit me often, now that you have returned to Rhodes, and that we will become reacquainted."

"You are as gracious as you are beautiful," Korax responded, his voice strained by a tangle of feelings.

But he had no opportunity to sort his emotions, as Patrollos came up beside Berenicea's couch. Cimon and Lyceas followed him, but not Amynias.

"I believe you've already met my friend Patrollos and his companions," Berenicea said.

Korax nodded to them, his expression carefully neutral.

"I am glad to see you here," Patrollos declared. "I hope we will have a chance to speak later, in private."

"Indeed," Berenicea said. "There will be ample time for friendly conversation. But now I know our poets are eager to begin. Please avail yourselves of a couch and some refreshments."

Korax wandered back across the floor and settled at the place Staphylus had saved for him. Servants ambled through the room, serving cups of wine, fruit, and assorted delicacies. Korax accepted a shallow wine bowl, but set it down without drinking.

Berenicea formally welcomed her guests. She invoked the blessings of Helios and Aphrodite and poured a libation to the Muses. Next, Staphylus walked to the center of the floor. Strumming his lyre, he opened the salon by introducing the evening's first performer.

A lady named Praxinoa, tall and gifted with a strong, high voice, sang a composition in praise of Helios. She was followed by

Machaon, a bearded man of middle age, who recited an ode in honor of the navy men lost at the Battle of Karpathos.

"What do you think of our little society so far?" Staphylus asked, anxious of Korax's opinion. "Of course, I know there is no comparison to the salons of Alexandria."

Korax smiled to reassure him. "Actually, I find the plainer diction and direct style of these Rhodian poets has much to commend it."

"Really?" Staphylus beamed. "I am so gratified."

But in truth, Korax was listening with only part of his attention. His moody gaze kept wandering back to Berenicea with a bittersweet fascination, then sweeping guardedly to observe Patrollos and Amynias. He was relieved when the intermission came and he was able to escape to the cool of the balcony. Leaning on the balustrade, he gazed down pensively into the dim, lush garden.

But presently Berenicea approached him, with Patrollos on her arm. Turning to them, Korax saw that Amynias, Cimon, and Lyceas had also come out.

"I hope you are enjoying yourself," Berenicea said.

"Indeed, lady. Your hospitality is wonderful, and your home is lovely."

Patrollos roughly cleared his throat. "I want to welcome you back to Rhodes, Korax. I hope we can forget our past troubles and make peace. Will you take my hand in friendship?"

After a moment's hesitation, Korax clasped Patrollos by the wrist. "As I told my cousin Amynias, I am willing to forget what was done in anger. I provoked you cruelly, Patrollos, and the next morning, you gave me a thorough beating. Both acts were done in the wildness of youth. If what happened that morning is the only cause for quarrel between us, then we are friends."

Instantly, he perceived that Patrollos understood his meaning. The man dropped his gaze and his handshake went slack.

"What other quarrel could there be, cousin?" Amynias inquired smoothly.

Korax considered, then spoke evenly. "If there is nothing concealed in your hearts, then there is nothing."

In the awkward silence he read their faces: a flush of shame on Patrollos and Cimon, a sparkle of panic in Lyceas' eyes. Amynias scrutinized him with cool hate.

"You were away from us five years," Berenicea said to break the tension. "I understand you lived part of that time in Alexandria."

"That's right." Korax resumed the façade of relaxed sociability. "A wonderful city. All the marvelous tales of it are true."

They conversed about the Library and the poetry scene. Patrollos and the others stood listening uneasily, until Amynias inserted a remark.

"But you didn't spend all of your time with books. Plainly, you have not neglected your physical training."

"No. The city has an excellent gymnasium. Mostly I worked on swordsmanship and wrestling."

"Oh, Amynias has become quite a wrestler," Lyceas ventured. "At least, he throws me five times out of six."

"I've heard they teach a different style in Alexandria," Amynias said, "with throws derived from Egypt and Libya."

Korax smiled blandly. "Yes, it's true. I learned many new tricks in Alexandria."

"Perhaps you'll consent to wrestle me some time," Amynias responded. "We look to be about the same weight. You can show me your skills. That is, if you are not afraid to test your manhood."

Korax's smile vanished, and they stared into each other's eyes. "Actually, I would welcome the chance to throw you down."

Cimon and Lyceas sucked in breath with an audible hiss.

Amynias thrust out his chest. "Why not here and now? I see the lady's garden has a patch of soft grass. It would make an excellent circle."

"Amynias! What are you thinking?" Patrollos barked. "You would break the lady's hospitality."

"Not at all," Amynias responded, undeterred. "A friendly match between cousins. I'm sure the lady will not object, assuming Korax is as willing as I."

Korax's eyes blazed. Athene had warned him not to attack Amynias, but she also said he should defend himself. Surely, answering this challenge would not be breaking his pledge to the goddess. All his pent anger erupted to the surface. He relished the chance to take his feelings out on Amynias, to rub his cousin's smirking face in the dirt.

"Best of three falls," he said.

"This is madness," Patrollos interjected. "Berenicea, say the word and I will stop it."

But, though her cheeks were pale with tension, Berenicea wore a distant, distracted expression. "No. Let them wrestle in the garden if that is their will."

"Let's go then," Amynias said.

Korax followed him toward the stairs. Everyone on the terrace had heard the exchange, and the entire party streamed after the two opponents, voices rising with excitement. The crowd passed Staphylus at the door of the banquet room.

"What is this?" he cried. "What is happening?"

Chapter Nine

Amynias stalked across the garden, unfastening his belt and handing it to Lyceas. He removed his headband and slippers, then pulled the loose chiton over his head.

Instinct had made him challenge Korax, a wild inner prompting. Over the years, Amynias had learned to trust his instincts, especially when they urged him to take chances other men deemed outrageous. The trait reminded him of the recklessness he admired in Korax when they were younger. In fact, Amynias traced this change in himself to the attack on Korax and its aftermath. Prodded by instinct, he had seized control of the situation when Patrollos and the others stood paralyzed by panic. Perhaps in that moment, he had stolen some of the reckless courage from Korax's soul.

This willingness to obey his wild instincts had brought Amynias opportunities and successes beyond all expectation. But those same instincts warned him that Korax's return to Rhodos could turn the Fates against him, strip him of all his gains. That was why he had destroyed his cousin's letters when they propitiously fell into his hands.

Now, perhaps his instincts had gained him a chance to be rid of Korax once and for all. Amynias knew certain holds that, ruthlessly applied, could prove lethal. Fatal accidents did happen in the ring. And in an unlighted garden, with the witnesses half-drunk, the opportunity seemed ripe.

The guests formed a rough circle at the center of the lawn. The placid salon had been transformed in eager anticipation of more violent entertainment. Men laughed boisterously and shouted out wagers. Flute girls, courtesans and household slaves gathered with them to watch the fight. Amynias spied Patrollos and Berenicea standing in the background, and with them the fop Staphylus. Those three alone seemed averse to the spectacle.

Amynias stepped naked into the ring, where Korax already waited. The two cousins were similar in size and body type, long limbed, with lean and supple muscle. Amynias was a shade taller and wider in the shoulders.

"Ready," called Cimon, who had appointed himself referee.

The combatants leaned forward and positioned their hands on each other's neck and shoulders.

"And, begin!"

They grappled, feet circling, arms and shoulders straining. Amynias forced his way forward but Korax sidestepped, deftly restoring the balance.

They circled again.

"You should not have come back to Rhodes," Amynias whispered. "It may prove unlucky for you."

His threat, meant to check Korax's courage, had the opposite effect. Korax crossed his feet with dizzying speed and circled behind his foe, a maneuver he learned in Alexandria. With one arm wrapped around his cousin's waist, Korax tried to slip the other in front of the armpit and behind the neck. But Amynias sensed the move and locked both hands onto the reaching arm. He bent at the waist and twisted violently. Korax was flung over his cousin's hip and landed heavily on his back.

The spectators roared.

"Fall one to Amynias," Cimon proclaimed.

Korax shook his head clear and clambered to his feet.

"Come on," Amynias jeered. "Are you beaten already?"

Incited to rage, Korax charged. The wild attack was exactly what Amynias wanted. Timing it perfectly, he sprang sideways and thrust one arm against Korax's chest. The momentum spun them both partway around. Amynias got behind Korax and clamped his free arm over his cousin's throat. Now he had Korax in a death-hold, his arms locked together and with plenty of leverage. Grunting with effort, Amynias squeezed.

Korax flailed his arms, desperately seeking a grip. But with Amynias on his back, the most he could do was slap a shoulder or reach behind and touch a hip—There was nothing to grab. He could not draw breath. Remorselessly, Amynias was crushing his windpipe.

"I told you, you should not have come back," Amynias whispered through his teeth.

Korax recalled another trick he had learned in Alexandria. In the library at the Paneum, he once studied an Egyptian medical text that illustrated the nerves of the human body. Certain points, forcefully pressed, could cause a momentary weakening of the muscles. He had shown those points to a wrestling coach, who was delighted to learn of them. The two had practiced using the points over several afternoons.

Now Korax felt desperately along the vertebrae of Amynias' neck. Just to the side of where the spine joined the collarbone, he found a nerve and pushed in hard with two fingertips. Amynias gave a slight shudder and his arm slackened. Korax caught a shallow breath and thrust harder. The hold on his throat loosened. Korax seized Amynias' arm with both hands and heaved, doubling at the waist.

Amynias rolled over Korax's shoulder. He managed to land on his feet, though it twisted him severely. Korax still gripped the arm, and he yanked violently, trying to force a fall. But Amynias refused to go down. Instead, he took a half step back to support his weight and jerked to pull his arm free. At the same instant, Korax lunged with all his strength. The two forces combined to wrench

Amynias' arm in the opposite direction from his torso. Korax heard a brutal crack as the shoulder tore from its socket.

Amynias unleashed a terrible scream and fell writhing onto his back. Korax stumbled to the edge of the circle and bent over, gasping for air. His neck felt wrenched and his throat bruised, but he seemed otherwise unhurt.

Cimon and Lyceas rushed forward to tend to Amynias. They shouted that the joint was dislocated and struggled with him, trying to hold him down and force it back into place. Patrollos pushed through the crowd to assist them.

The rest of the party milled about, muttering uneasily or paying off wagers. Korax looked up to find Staphylus standing over him.

"Are you hurt?"

Korax shook his head.

"Well, I think you are the winner," Staphylus remarked. "And I think I need some strong wine. I will bring you some."

As he walked away, the air was rent by another grisly scream. It appeared Cimon and Patrollos had succeeded in putting the joint back in place, but perhaps only part way. They faced each other, and Patrollos shook his head dubiously. Amynias lay unconscious at their feet.

"We'd best get him to a physician," Patrollos said.

Patrollos leaned over, and Cimon and Lyceas together lifted the inert Amynias onto his back. While Cimon made sure the load was balanced, Lyceas scurried off to retrieve Amynias' clothing. Patrollos paused for a brief, regretful word with Berenicea. Then he carried his burden across the courtyard and out the gate, Lyceas and Cimon on his heels.

Berenicea calmly stepped forward and asked for everyone's attention. "My friends, I think it best we reconvene the salon on another evening. I fear the Muses have been frightened away by the fierce spirit of Ares, the god of war."

She strolled back inside, followed by several attendants. The rest of her staff ambled off to assist the guests in collecting their cloaks and sandals.

Korax dressed gingerly. By the time he had put on his headband, Staphylus had reappeared with two tumblers of dark red wine. They wished each other good health and drank it down.

"You must come to the salon again," Staphylus said dryly. "You bring a certain excitement we're not used to."

Korax chuckled ruefully but could think of no reply.

When they stopped at the antechamber by the gate, a slave brought Staphylus his footgear and himation. But one of the black-haired courtesans awaited Korax.

"My lady Berenicea asks that you permit me to bathe you. Then, if you will do her the honor of joining her upstairs, she wishes to apologize for the unfortunate breach of her hospitality."

Korax glanced uncertainly at Staphylus, who immediately bowed. "I will call on you tomorrow to see that you are well."

The woman conducted Korax to a tiled bathroom with warm and cold pools. She sponged his body in the heated water, dried him with a thick towel, rubbed him with hot, scented oil. Dressed in a clean linen chiton and corded belt, Korax followed her up the central staircase.

Berenicea received him in an airy chamber beyond the banquet hall. Couches and cushioned chairs were spread across the floor and the adjacent balcony. Perfumed oil burned in delicate lamps, casting a soft, fluttering glow. Berenicea had changed into a white gown bound at the shoulders with silver pins. Her hair was loose and fell like a thick veil down her back.

"I am happy you consented to see me." She handed him a silver goblet. "I hope you are not hurt."

"Not seriously." Korax stood close, his eyes drinking her in. "You have nothing to apologize for, dear hostess. It was Amynias' doing, and my own."

"Still, I regret that it happened. I wonder now if I should have let Patrollos stop you."

"Why didn't you?"

Her eyes, which had stayed fixed on his since his entry, now shifted away. She glanced out at her garden.

"Because the goddess whispered to me that I should not interfere, that this was something fated between Amynias and you."

Suddenly the lovely hetaera seemed even more intriguing. "Does the goddess whisper to you often?"

She eyed him shyly. "When I need her to, or when she requires a service of me. I am her priestess. We consecrated our temple to her a year ago in the spring."

She sank onto a divan and gestured for Korax to join her.

He sat down, carefully leaving a space between them. "I knew the Temple of Aphrodite was finished," he said. "I did not know you were a priestess."

"Yes." She eyed him, smiling. "A young man steered me onto that path, one of my first loves. He sang a hymn to Aphrodite, in which he said he saw her light in me. That night, I started to feel how she truly does dwell in me, and to believe I could become more than a simple slave girl. Lady Emerine honored my aspirations. She trained me in the priestess craft, and when the temple was dedicated, she gave me my freedom."

Korax quivered inside. "I am glad my song could have such an effect. For me, the outcome of that night was not so lucky."

"I know what happened to you the next morning. I am so sorry."

"Perhaps that too was fated," Korax murmured. "Certainly, I was partly to blame."

"Patrollos regrets that he harmed you. I think the guilt of it has haunted him ever since."

"Patrollos, yes." Korax stared at the floor. "He is your lover now. Did you invite me here to speak on his behalf?"

"No. I invited you here because I wanted to."

Korax observed the smile on her lips. He found himself smiling in return, while his body made its own involuntary response to her. But then his gaze returned to the floor, and he shook his head.

"I would be glad to find forgiveness in my heart. But there is more than a beating among youths involved—other things that are harder to forgive."

She looked bewildered. "What other things?"

Korax set down his goblet and stood. "I'll leave Patrollos tell you that, if he wishes."

She reached for his hand. "You are angry with me?"

"No, dear Berenicea. For you, there is only admiration and tenderness in my heart."

She peered up at him. "Yet, you have decided not to stay."

Korax considered. He had not felt so drawn to a woman since … The very thought of Kalyssa made him release Berenicea's hand.

"It is best that I go. I would not wish to make Patrollos jealous."

"That is not a concern. Patrollos knows I am free to love anyone I choose." She had stood and now searched his eyes. "There is another reason, a truer reason. Someone has broken your heart."

Korax bowed his head. "You are perceptive. It will mend in time, I am sure."

"Oh, my dear friend." Berenicea clasped both his hands. Korax could feel her sympathy, affection, and yearning as though they were his own emotions.

"If I can help it mend, please come to me. As you may know, I do not charge money, only accept gifts. But you have already given me the most worthwhile gift of my life. I would never ask anything of you, except a chance to repay it."

Korax could not speak. He bowed low and left the lady's chamber.

Chapter Ten

Korax woke in the night, his neck hurting as though he had been beaten with a cudgel. He shifted and turned in the bed, but could find no position that wasn't painful. Finally he sprawled on his back, staring at the dim ceiling.

"I did warn you to beware of Amynias." Athene's voice came to him.

"Are you saying I should have refused his challenge?"

"That might have been wiser. But no, given the provocation, I cannot fault you for fighting him. Perhaps it was fated, as the priestess of Aphrodite observed."

Closing his eyes, Korax had a fleeting vision: his destiny and that of Amynias, two spiraling streams of force, preordained to clash again and again.

"It would seem to be so," Athene said. "Amynias has now shown that his intentions are murderous. He was badly injured, but he will not be deterred. Indeed, the pain and humiliation will only enflame his hate. But he has also learned that rash action will not succeed. Now, I expect he will revert to his natural tendencies—cunning and treachery."

"In those skills he is a master," Korax remarked with fatalistic gloom. "What is your counsel?"

"I believe some of your books contain magic for protection against evil. It might be well to perform such rites. Also, the amulet that your friend Miriam gave you: I would be sure to wear it."

"Oh, Amynias! That looks horrible, just horrible!" Epiteleia's elaborate earrings jingled and shimmered as her head shook with dismay. "Your shoulder is as purple and swollen as an overripe melon. How can I bear such a grievous injury to my child?"

She sat down heavily beside him, jarring the bed frame and bringing a grunt of pain from Amynias. He leaned against a pile of cushions, naked under a linen sheet. The injured shoulder was bare, the arm bound tightly against his torso by bandages.

"How could this have happened?" Epiteleia cried. "You've seen the physician? What did he say?"

"It was a wrestling injury, mother. Neshicles says it will heal in time."

"Wrestling! I've told you so often to be careful wrestling. Why do my children never listen to me? And why didn't you call for me? You know I would have come at once. Instead I had to hear the news from your gatekeeper Eriphon—that ugly, crooked little man."

"I did not wish to worry you," Amynias replied with barely concealed exasperation. "Besides, there is nothing you can do. Neshicles said it needs rest. There is no other remedy."

"Nonsense! Your mother's loving care will speed your cure." She patted his knee comfortingly. "I will stay right here till you are better. I will send porters to my house and have a few things brought over. I will take the bedroom next to yours."

Amynias' eyes widened with alarm. "No, mother. I would not put you to such trouble."

"My brave boy! Always thinking of others instead of yourself. You get that trait from me, I know. But a person can carry unselfishness too far. No, a mother has certain duties, and I am determined not to neglect them. I will stay as long as you need me—even though it is a beautiful day, and I was planning to spend the afternoon at the Temple of Hermes."

Epiteleia belonged to the ladies' guild at the temple, an affiliation that permitted her to spend her afternoons with other wealthy widows of the town, gossiping and playing draughts or the board game called 'five-line.' Sometimes her gambling losses were astonishing. Still, to Amynias' mind, the guild kept his mother from other trouble and, more importantly, from bothering him.

He gripped her wrist firmly with his good hand. "Listen to me carefully, mother. I sincerely prefer that you go on with your normal activities and not concern yourself with me. I will heal most quickly with plenty of rest, and with the knowledge that you are content."

Epiteleia appeared both crestfallen and relieved. "Well, if you are sure you feel that way. Naturally, I only want to do what is best for you."

She bustled out a short time later, vowing to stop in every day to visit and make sure his slaves were caring for him properly.

Amynias breathed a sigh of gratitude when she was gone. Wincing, he tried to work the hand and fingers of his damaged arm. In speaking to his mother, he had underplayed the severity of the injury. Old Neshicles had declared it the gravest kind of shoulder separation, nerves and blood vessels badly torn. He refused to speculate to what extent it would heal.

But Amynias was determined to recover fully and soon. He would not go through life with a crippled arm, especially not by his cousin's doing. And he would revenge himself on Korax in time— this he swore. He had underestimated his despicable cousin, but even so had nearly crushed him. Next time, he would plan more carefully.

He had more visitors in the afternoon. Amynias straightened on the cushions as Lyceas, Cimon, and Patrollos were ushered into the bedroom. They peered down at him solemnly, and tried to mask their pity and revulsion with hearty greetings.

Amynias showed an equally sanguine demeanor. "My friends, I must thank you all for getting me to the physician so quickly.

Neshicles informed me this morning that any delay would have made the injury that much harder to mend."

"How are you feeling?" Lyceas asked.

"Sore. But I am resolved on a speedy recovery."

Patrollos stood awkwardly at the bedside. "Cimon and I are due back at our ship tomorrow. Is there anything you need that we can do for you today?"

"Don't worry about that," Lyceas said. "I will see he is cared for, and I will deliver his work as soon as he is able. My father is already asking when you will be fit enough to take on your accounts again."

"Soon." Amynias' voice turned hoarse and bitter. "I will not let my cousin's vile trickery disrupt my life."

The remark caused an uncomfortable hush to settle. But then Patrollos spoke.

"Don't you think you brought it on yourself, Amynias? It was supposed to be a harmless poetry reading. What madness compelled you to start a fight?"

Amynias gazed at the black tree limbs outside his window. "Madness! It must have been .... Don't you see? It must have been Korax's arts. He bewitched me into challenging him."

Cimon and Lyceas shuffled their feet and glanced about with superstitious unease.

Patrollos glared. "No, Amynias. You challenged him of your own volition."

"Do you think so? Do you think I could be so ill-mannered a guest? That I would act so outlandishly of my own will? No. I was befuddled by sorcery—It's the only explanation. Korax has not forgiven us. He knows, or at least suspects, that we did more than give him a beating. You all heard what he said."

"Yes." Lyceas nodded stonily. *"If there is nothing concealed in our hearts to make us enemies* ... Amynias is right. Somehow Korax knows that we bribed the pirates."

"I know what he said," Patrollos answered. "And I also know what I saw during the match. You put a death-hold on him, Amynias. You tried to murder him."

Amynias saw no gain in denying it. "I tried to snuff out the life of an evil sorcerer." He pointed to his ruined shoulder. "You see the result. I warn you, my friends: we are not safe. We are all in desperate danger."

"What should we do?" Lyceas asked.

"No!" Patrollos declared vehemently. "He will lead us into more treachery and dishonor. I will not go down that road with you again, Amynias. I swear it before the gods."

Amynias lifted his eyebrows. "Then what will you do? Confess your crimes to Korax? Plead for his mercy? I do not advise it."

Patrollos hesitated, backed into a corner. "I will say nothing to Korax. But nor will I help with any more of your schemes."

Amynias hid his relief. He did not need Patrollos' aid, only his continued silence. "Go back to your ship, Patrollos. I do not ask your help. I will deal with my cousin, in my own way and my own time. But I warn you this: Do not interfere with me, and never speak about Korax's ransom to anyone."

They gazed at one another with undisguised malice. At last, Patrollos whirled and stalked out of the room. Hesitant and fearful, Cimon followed.

Amynias turned to Lyceas, who watched him with a look of awe.

Since Zeno was forced to reduce the size of his household, the planting in his courtyard had suffered serious neglect. Weeds and nettles choked the flowerbeds, withered ferns drooped from vases, and vines reached untrammeled up columns and walls.

Kleis, the upstairs cleaning maid, took it on herself to remedy the problem. She had grown up in a farming community in the highlands of western Italia, a region known for its rich soil and flowering meadows. She found the decay of Zeno's garden more depressing than she could bear.

So, when her other chores allowed, Kleis frequently went out to the courtyard in apron and sun-hat. Kneeling in the soil or bending over the stone pots, she dug out the weeds and staked and watered the flowers and herbs she wished to cultivate.

One hot afternoon, she wrestled with a dense patch of ivy that had grown up one wall of the courtyard. Kleis was a tall girl, and stronger than her willowy figure might have suggested. She found it easy enough to tear the vines from the masonry. But plucking the tough, obdurate roots was another matter.

While she struggled with the task, Leukon sat nearby on the rim of a dry fountain. At his feet, the Celt had spread a scroll from the library of his master Korax. But Leukon spent less time perusing the lines of verse than he did staring off with a blank, forlorn expression.

Kleis kept hoping Leukon would notice her efforts and come to her aid. She made a blatant display of grunting and huffing over the difficult work. Leukon aloofly ignored her.

Finally, Kleis could take it no longer. "You ought to be helping me, you know."

The Celt appeared not to have heard.

"You, Leukon! You ought to help me with this, you know."

He turned to her, the remote countenance settling into a frown of puzzlement. "I am not a slave of the house."

"No, but you live here. You eat from Zeno's table like the rest of us. It is certainly fair to ask that you do a little work—especially when you're stronger than all of us put together. The garden is not my responsibility either. I'm only trying to make the house more pleasant and beautiful for everyone."

Leukon seemed to ponder her arguments. Then he shook his head decisively. "I am a warrior. My dignity does not allow me to scratch in the dirt like a farmer."

His statement enraged Kleis. She marched over to him and set her hands on her hips. "O mighty warrior, please forgive me for daring to suggest that you lift one of your mighty fingers to earn your keep! But of course, that would interfere with you sitting on your mighty rump all day brooding and pretending to read books."

Leukon gaped at the infuriated, sweating woman. Unabashedly, he grinned. "You are a lovely girl. This agitation becomes you."

As his words sank in, her eyes widened. "Oh!" She smacked him hard on the upper arm and stamped off to resume her work.

Leukon returned to his reading. But now he found Kleis' constant muttering and whimpering a distraction. He looked up from the scroll several times. As he watched her struggle, his brow furrowed and his mouth twisted as if he pondered some deep, internal conflict. He jerked halfway to his feet, then sat down again. Finally, he set his jaw and rose in a fluid motion. He walked stealthily over to Kleis and crouched beside her.

He shook a forefinger in front of her nose. "If you ever meet anyone of my tribe, you will not speak of this."

He wrapped his huge hand around a vine and ripped it easily from the soil.

Kleis eyed him with appreciation and amazement. "By the bones of Heracles, you are strong!"

The mole of the main harbor stretched over a half-mile, a long bulwark shielding the western flank of the bay from the open sea. On top of the mole was a walkway and, at the end, a rounded parapet where the priests of Poseidon came sometimes to offer sacrifice.

On the evening of a dark moon, Korax walked alone to the end of the mole. He wore a hooded blue cloak trimmed in silver and carried a wineskin and a ceremonial dagger. On his chest was the amulet Miriam had designed.

In the past month, two more cargos from Rhodos had been stolen by pirates. Worse, word reached the town that the family's vessel, the *Melancarmia*, had sunk in a storm off Locri. Korax had decided he must speak with the god of the sea.

Behind him, the last remnant of daylight died over the city. All around him surged the gray, unquiet waters. He climbed onto the parapet wall and pulled the stopper from the wineskin. Whispering words of offering, he poured the wine onto the rocks below.

Returning to the center of the parapet, he drew his dagger and traced a magic circle in the air, an invisible boundary of protection. Next, he drew the sigil of Poseidon, then of Set, the Egyptian god of the abyss.

He spread out his arms and spoke his summons: "Poseidon, son of Kronos, tamer of horses, earth-shaker, lord of the sea, accept my humble offering in peace and deign to speak with me. Arise from your golden palace beneath the waves and come into my presence, mighty lord."

He waited. After a time, a gust of wind lifted his cloak. The nocturnal sea surrounded him like an enormous living spirit, a god of old and dreadful power.

"Mortal man of Rhodes, I know you. You have sought to pierce my intentions with your tiny mind. Now you would cajole my will with a meager spilling of wine?"

The voice, compounded of wind and wave, reverberated to the bottom of Korax's soul, where it roused an instinctual terror. Korax lowered his arms, pressed his feet firmly on the rock.

"Mighty Poseidon, I am in truth but a puny mortal, and have no wish to rouse your enmity. I only ask what I can do, what the men of Rhodes can do, to appease your wrath and secure your protection."

The wind blew harder, salt stinging his eyes.

"Of old, three sons were born to my father Kronos, the devourer of his children. When we gods overthrew Kronos and chained his body to the pillars of the world, we divided his realm into three. Zeus took the sky, Hades the underworld, and the sea became mine to rule. Earth and Olympus, we agreed to hold in joint and equal dominion. But now on earth and sea alike, men disdain my worship. Those who do offer prayers and sacrifices make empty gestures; the awe and fear have dwindled in their hearts. I will not succor them."

Korax lifted his chin and answered, "It is true that many men have lost their belief in the old gods. But the seafarers of Rhodes still honor you with all due reverence. I have sailed with them, and I know this to be true."

"I will not debate my whims and actions with you—I am a god! I will make the waves crash and the storms blow as the urges strike me. So it has always been and will always be. As for the sea-wolves, the men of Crete worship me with fitting veneration. I will not scorn their sacrifices, nor will I help the Rhodians destroy them."

Now the wind was howling. Back along the mole, Korax could see the spume of waves splashing on the rocks. He saw no further point in trying to placate the sea god. He only wished to end the audience and withdraw himself to safety.

"Mighty Poseidon, tamer of horses, earth-shaker, lord of the sea: I thank you for your presence here at the boundary of your realm. To pay you further homage, I will make worthy sacrifice at your temple."

He bowed low and stayed down. Gradually the wind died away and the powerful immanence dissipated. Korax rose and quelled his fear with long, deliberate breaths.

The sky was starless. Across the harbor, the braziers and lanterns of the city cast the only feeble light. Korax picked his way warily back along the mole, pressed on both sides by the dark and sinister sea, feeling defeated and utterly alone.

Chapter Eleven

Among the most prominent of the ruling families was the House of Philophron, of which Halitherses was the current lord. His mansion, one of the oldest and grandest houses in Rhodos, sat low on the hill of the town overlooking the temples and government halls. Within its courtyard stretched a stately garden planted with bougainvillea, cypress, and myrtle.

One warm afternoon in late summer, Amynias entered the garden gate and paced along the edge of a long reflecting pool. At the top of the garden, Thalia awaited him on a wrought-iron bench. At a discreet distance from her, but within plain sight, two woman-servants of the house sat over their needlework. This arrangement was a compromise between the old custom, in which a betrothed couple hardly met before the wedding, and the freer habits of the current day—which had permitted Thalia to get herself into so much trouble.

Amynias bowed to his future bride and took her hand to kiss. His left arm, tightly bandaged, remained hidden beneath his himation.

"You look lovely as ever, my dear Thalia."

"Then why haven't you come to visit me lately? I have not seen you in almost two months."

Frowning, Amynias lifted his eyes to the statue that loomed over the pool, a stern bronze warrior on a marble plinth. This was the noble Philophron, one of the founders of Rhodos. Allying himself with that bloodline was the chief reason Amynias sought to marry Thalia.

"Forgive me, I did not mean to sound so selfish," she said. "I know you have been ill. I heard about your accident."

"Yes. Between business and the regimens to recover my strength, I've had little leisure."

In truth, Amynias had spent many extra hours at the gymnasium. Only the suggestion of recovery was misleading. Despite all his dogged, painful exercising, the forearm had shriveled, and he could barely move the hand. The physicians merely shook their heads and concluded the damage was probably permanent. Amynias vented his rage and frustration by incessantly casting the javelin. Even with only one good arm, he was becoming quite expert—for he imagined every straw target to be the naked torso of his cursed cousin.

"You shoulder is still not better?" Thalia asked with concern.

Amynias shifted his eyes. "It is taking longer to heal than I had hoped."

"Can you show me?"

"It is best not to remove the bandages."

"Oh, of course." Thalia bit her lip. "It *is* getting better though?"

Amynias smiled smoothly. "Dear Thalia, I promise, by our wedding day my limbs will be quite sound—and fully capable of tossing you around our bed."

Thalia laughed shyly and blushed, seemingly reassured.

Well enough, Amynias thought. If he had not healed by then, the little sow would just have to choose between marrying a cripple and suffering the scandal of yet another failed betrothal. He hardly cared. By then he would have other satisfactions: by then his scheme for punishing Korax would have borne fruit. That plot was developing beautifully, and imagining its sweet success absorbed Amynias more and more.

As the summer waned, Zeno's courtyard was gradually transformed from a bleak wilderness to a tidy, flourishing garden.

With Leukon's daily help, Kleis ripped down the overgrown vines, pulled weeds and dead stalks, and pruned the trees and hedges. New roses climbed on freshly-painted trellises, and green parsley and purple lavender spilled out of tiled beds.

As the days cooled, Kleis grew more ambitious. She and Leukon dug out a row of thorny acanthus and planted lily and gladiolus bulbs. She seeded grape vines and, taking advantage of Leukon's prodigious strength, coaxed him to move and rearrange the fig trees in their huge stone pots.

One day in mid-autumn, Korax heard them through an open casement of the upstairs corridor. Kleis had sent Leukon up a ladder with a pruning saw to trim the branches of a tall tree. She called out to him repeatedly to be careful of falling.

"Kleis, stop worrying," Leukon answered in his booming voice. "I scaled much higher ladders in King Ptolemy's army, while training to besiege cities. And here, no fat sergeants are tossing stones down at my head."

Distracted from his work by their banter and the noise of the saw, Korax finally walked out to the corridor and closed the casement. He did not begrudge their enjoyment of each other. Indeed, he had noticed with relief when Leukon took up the relationship with Kleis. Since she put him to work in the garden, Leukon seemed far less moody and frustrated. These days, Korax seldom saw the Celt's woeful, brooding visage. Naturally, Korax had foreseen that the couple would end up in bed—he did not begrudge them that either. When Menas, the peevish and surly steward of the house, complained about Kleis' licentious behavior to Zeno, Korax convinced his uncle to discreetly ignore the affair. The generous-hearted Zeno readily agreed. Kleis was a pleasant and dutiful servant, and Zeno saw no reason to deny her this happiness. Besides, everyone was enjoying the improved condition of the garden.

Korax slumped back into his room and shut the door. The wide chamber was crowded with tables and the tables cluttered with vestiges of his many tasks: papyrus rolls and sheets, ink pots and styluses, candles, wax carvings, incense burners and magical tools.

On one tabletop lay a mortar and pestle, sealed jars and bunches of dried herbs. Korax had purchased the goods from a Phoenician dealer in the Rhodos emporium. He used them to concoct an ointment that he rubbed each morning on his father's eyes. Korax had never studied the healing arts in any depth, but when he found a remedy for failing eyesight in one of his books, he decided he must try. At first, Leontes balked at the idea, and Korax did not press him. But after a few days, the old man mentioned the ointment of his own accord and asked to try it. That was a month ago. Leontes did claim he was seeing a little better now, though Korax was not entirely convinced.

In a listless mood, he wandered out to his balcony. An overcast sky hung over Rhodos, and the sea was leaden. The sailing season had ended and the long docks were crowded with ships. More freighters lay anchored in the harbor. Already, some vessels had been dragged into dry-dock for the winter.

Korax counted it lucky that only three of the family's cargos had been lost to pirates. Even with the sinking of the *Melancarmia*, most of the ventures Zeno had put money in would bring returns. The family could pay its debts and stay in business for another year. Apparently, Korax's magical protections had succeeded, at least to some degree. From all accounts, many of the merchants of Rhodos had fared worse.

He turned and stepped back into his chamber. He sat down at his writing table and attempted to focus his mind. He was composing the formulas for a spell of protection. Athene had advised him to perform such workings, to ward off whatever evil

Amynias was planning. Korax had been trying to finish the spell for days.

But as he reviewed the instructions in the text, the Egyptian characters filed before his eyes in a bizarre and meaningless parade. He set down the stylus and rubbed his eyelids. Overwork had taken its toll, left him exhausted—the endless hours poring over the map and wax ships, mentally struggling against the merciless, inexorable sea god.

But it was more than that. Magical power derived from the will, and will found its source in the emotional nature, the passions of the soul. In Memphis, his will had been spurred by the thirst for freedom, in Alexandria, by his adoration of Kalyssa. In Rhodos duty, the love of family and city, had driven him. But those wells were overdrawn and running dry. His powers were starting to fail.

He considered summoning Athene. But though he venerated the goddess and devotedly sought her counsel, her presence did not nourish his spirit. Not in the way he needed. Instead, he lay down on his bed and stared out at the gray and windy sky.

He was still lying there an hour or two later when Phoemio called him for dinner. Korax sent the slave away without opening the door. He felt a deep and aching hunger, but it was nothing food or wine would satisfy.

Suddenly, he made a decision. Afraid he might change his mind, he moved quickly, putting on sandals and cloak, descending the stairs and leaving the house through the front gate.

The north wind was blowing, gusty and wet, and raindrops splattered on the cobbles. Though it was just twilight, the sky in the north hovered dark and threatening. The rain fell harder as Korax climbed the high, murky streets.

He came within sight of Berenicea's house then stopped. A few lamps burned in the upper story, but there was no way to tell if the lady was home. Besides, he had not sent a note to ask if he might call. It would be the height of discourtesy to show up unannounced on her doorstep, drenched and disheveled like a stray puppy in the storm.

No, he could not be so rude.

He hurried past her house, through the battering wind and falling curtains of rain. He took refuge nearby, in the deserted arcade of the theater. Leaning against a damp wall, he watched the rain make puddles and rivulets in the street. Since the unfortunate wrestling match with Amynias, Korax has not gone to recitals or parties. With only work and study to fill his days, he missed the friendships he enjoyed in Alexandria. Most of all, he missed the intimacy of a lover.

Abruptly, he found himself walking again, marching resolutely through the night. Without pausing to weigh his actions or consider what he would say, he went to the front of Berenicea's house and pounded on the door.

After some time, the burly gatekeeper opened it a crack. Holding up his lantern, he peered at Korax warily.

"I know the hour is late," Korax said, "but is your lady at home? Does she have a visitor?"

He gave the man his name and waited, the steady rain dripping from his soaked garments. Presently the gate opened wide, and he was conducted into the house. Two handmaids removed his wet clothes and dried him with towels. They clothed him in a clean chiton and led him up the stairs.

Berenicea awaited him in her sitting room, dressed in a robe of dark green silk. Her blue eyes shone in the gleam of a scented lamp.

"My friend, I am so happy you are here. I have ordered hot spiced wine for us to drink."

She reached out her hands but Korax, still not pausing, not weighing his actions, embraced her and laid his forehead on her shoulder. In a moment, he was sobbing like a babe.

Berenicea stroked his hair, her voice a tearful sigh. "Oh, my dear, I know. I know. You have been forced to wander far and suffer many sorrows. But all that is over now. You are home at last, in the arms of one who loves you."

Chapter Twelve

On a wet cloudy day, Korax and Leontes paid a visit to the tomb of Anticleia. Korax's mother was interred in the family's ancestral vault, in the necropolis outside the city walls. Leontes rode on the back of a donkey, which Korax led through the streets. It was the first time in two years the old man had ventured from Zeno's house.

Inside a mausoleum of gray brick, a steep narrow stair led to the underground tomb. Korax helped his father down the steps, then made a second trip to bring the offerings—a wreath of myrtle, bread and wine.

The urn holding Anticleia's ashes was set on a shelf in the mausoleum wall. The shelf was sealed by a monument stone etched with an inscription:

Anticleia lies here. She loved her children as strongly as mortal can love, and in all ways was a dutiful wife to Leontes, whose grief at her loss is boundless.

"I can read the lines," Leontes said, holding up a lantern and leaning close to the stone. "That concoction of yours is certainly helping my vision."

"I am glad, father."

The lantern rattled in his hand. "Oh, the words bring back all the pain of that time. Help me to sit down, Korax."

Korax assisted his father to a seat at the opposite wall of the vault. Then he placed the wreath before the grave and poured a libation. Standing with head bowed, he whispered to his mother's spirit. He thanked her for the sacrifices she had made, for she had given him life not once but twice. And he thanked her for the guidance and protection she had lavished on him, even from the world of the dead.

"After all this time," Leontes muttered, "the grief still is raw."

Korax crossed the vault and knelt before his father. "She watches over us. Not just here, but every moment of every day. Her spirit has rescued me more than once. She has not abandoned you, father."

Leontes squeezed his hand. "My son, you have been most kind and patient to an old man. I am so sorry I was cruel to you and did not welcome you fairly when you came home."

"It is forgotten."

"And I must thank you also for helping Zeno. I do not know how we would have managed this year without you. But wait, I have more to say. Will you listen to the advice of your father?"

"Of course I will."

"I worry that you work too much, between the business and your studies. It is so easy to miss the essential things in life, as I did with you and your mother. Do not make the same mistake, Korax. Find a good wife and marry, and if the gods bless you with children, spend as many hours with your family as you possibly can. Make them the center of your heart and all your attention. Do not waste that precious gift as I did, consumed with work and money."

Korax caressed the old man's face. "I do not know when I will be ready or fit to marry. But I promise, I will take your words into my heart."

Arriving home, they found Zeno's house in an uproar. Phoemio opened the gate, his swarthy face creased with dismay.

"Thank the Goddess you are back, masters. Zeno is waiting for you inside. Go, I will take care of the donkey."

"What is the problem?" Korax demanded.

"Oh, terrible news. Terrible," was all Phoemio would say. He grabbed the donkey's reins and headed off to return the beast to the stables.

Korax guided his father through the courtyard and into the house. Zeno sat in the foyer beside Callipatria, who was crying. Zeno's son, Isochomachus, home from sea for the winter, paced angrily. Zeno jumped up from the couch, waving a papyrus.

"There you are, Korax. Have a look at this!" Zeno thrust the document in front of his face.

"What is it? What is the trouble?" Leontes bawled.

"Help my father to sit." Korax passed the old man's arm to Isochomachus, who shuffled him over to the couch.

Korax unrolled the papyrus. It was a notice from the Magistrates' Court of Rhodos.

"You see," Zeno shouted before Korax could read any further. "Amynias has charged you with sorcery. And the scoundrel implicates me as well!"

Korax held the sheet in trembling hands. The indictment charged him with using witchcraft to protect the family's shipping ventures and cursing the ships of other merchants. It also accused him of bewitching Amynias into a wrestling match and then doing him grave injury. The charges were supported by claims that Korax's mother was a known Thracian witch, and that he had studied magic in Egypt. The indictment stated that he set up magical apparatus and performed acts of sorcery in the house of his uncle Zeno, who was therefore named an accomplice.

"This is insanity," Korax declared. "Some of the details are true, but not the charges. They are compounded of evil interpretations and outright lies. There can be no evidence to prove them. Yet it says there are witnesses."

"There is Menas for one," Zeno answered. "Our steward is nowhere to be found. Apparently he spied on us and now has fled to Amynias for refuge. If that is so, he is a treacherous knave. No doubt he will swear to whatever lies Amynias tells him to speak."

"How could Amynias do this to us?" Callipatria wailed. "He is our kinsman, our own nephew."

"Because he is a deceiver and a bloodsucker," Zeno shouted. "Better my cousin Callias had never married that Carian she-wolf Epiteleia. Better Amynias had been exposed at birth."

Korax stared at the papyrus, straining to comprehend the implications. Enough of the circumstances were true that, with a witness or two to give incriminating testimony, he might actually be convicted. He was no expert in Rhodian law, but the penalty for crimes involving witchcraft must be forfeiture of property and exile at least—more likely death.

"What are we to do, Korax?" Isochomachus demanded. "I'd like to string Amynias up by his heels, but I realize rough seaman's justice won't help us here."

"He has ruined us," Leontes moaned in a frail, hopeless voice. "Amynias has ruined us all at last."

"No he hasn't," Korax said. "I don't know how, but I will defeat him. And I will make him eat his lies."

"Bright-eyed goddess, grant me your wise counsel."

"I am here with you, Korax of Rhodes."

"I need your aid most sorely. My family and my very life are threatened. Can you advise me how to thwart Amynias?"

"You need a counselor who is wise in the Rhodian law—perhaps your friend Staphylus."

"I've already thought of him. Zeno hates all lawyers and distrusts the ones he has hired in the past. I think he will agree to consult with Staphylus. But is there no more you can tell me?"

"Amynias has spied on you and your family. I think it time you returned the favor. He hides many things. If you can expose them, you may be able to turn his treachery against him."

"Yes, that is good advice. I will endeavor to learn his secrets."

"And I counsel one other thing: Do not neglect to visit Berenicea. Her love sustains your heart. But more than that, she is allied with my sister goddess. Aphrodite may be able to help you in ways of her own."

Late that night, Korax sat on a carpet in the center of his chamber, a scrying bowl in his lap.

At first, he stirred water with a little wine. With this, he perceived visions of Amynias in his house, at the gymnasium, walking in the streets. But there was nothing out of the ordinary, nothing of any use.

Korax emptied the bowl and poured a new mixture, adding droplets of oil and tinctures of powder from tiny flasks. Now he glimpsed more private moments: Amynias meeting with clients at his bank in the Emporium, caressing a courtesan at a drinking party. And Korax began to sense the presence of secrets, clandestine dealings with shadowy men. But he could not picture these matters clearly.

Frustrated, he emptied the bowl and tried again, using the strongest scrying charm he knew. He held a needle in the flame of a lamp then pricked his finger with the red-hot point. He squeezed drops of blood into the water and stirred.

Yes, there was certainly more, much more to Amynias' business affairs than anyone in Rhodos suspected. Still these scenes were hidden, as though in banks of dense sea fog. No matter how deeply he concentrated, Korax's mind could not pierce the enigma. It reminded him of his inability to see Queen Arsinoe's plot in Alexandria, when Kalyssa's spell obscured his vision. But that made no sense, unless Amynias himself was practicing magic—or perhaps someone in league with him? Both possibilities seemed unlikely.

Korax opened his eyes and watched the clouds of incense curl and shimmer in the lamplight. He had to find another way to reveal Amynias' secrets. He stared blankly for a time, and then an obvious idea occurred.

He climbed to his feet and picked up one of the burning lamps on his way out of the room. He hurried downstairs to the slave quarters and knocked softly on Phoemio's door.

"I'm sorry to disturb you," he said, when Phoemio opened the door and peered at him groggily. "May I come in?"

"Of course, master."

The slave fetched a stool from against the wall and placed it in the middle of the tiny room. Korax sat and put his lamp on the nightstand. He regarded Phoemio in the shuddering light.

"I need to draw on your vast reserves of knowledge, my friend. What can you tell me of Amynias that I might not know already?"

"Well, that he is a scoundrel and villain you do know already, I am sure." Phoemio stroked his wrinkled brow. "Let me think ... He has five slaves in his household: Eriphon the gatekeeper; Apelles, who tends the garden and the downstairs; Stratola is his cook and a fine, fat woman of Sicilian blood. She is a much superior cook to our own Glauke—but please, never mention to Glauke that I said so. There is also Melite, who cleans the upstairs and makes the beds. Amynias beds her on occasion, or so I've gathered. That leaves Hicesius the accountant—you know him already. He's the Etruscan who used to belong to your father."

"What else?" Korax prompted.

"Well, Amynias does not entertain often—the miserly rascal. But he attends banquets and drinking parties aplenty at the houses of his wealthy friends. He exercises at the Diagoraseum—no public gymnasium for him. The only frequent visitor to his house that I know of is his mother. He cannot abide her, by all accounts. And who can blame him, for she is a most selfish and tiresome woman."

"What about his business dealings?" Korax pressed him. "I know he has a partnership in a bank."

"Yes, the House of Theadetus, I believe. Everyone knows Amynias has made quite a fortune for himself. He is said to have banking partners also in Cos and Caria, perhaps other places too. He's also bought a farmstead up in the highlands."

"That's odd," Korax mused. "I would not expect that sort of investment to interest him. He does not strike me as an aspiring landowner."

Phoemio shrugged. "That's really all I can think of. I'm sorry there is not more."

Korax gave a thoughtful nod. "See what else you can learn. Ask around in the marketplace, the Emporium, everywhere."

"Of course, master. Only, what should I be asking? What are we trying to find out?"

"Anything unusual, anything that might shed light on his associates and business concerns." Korax stood up, suddenly very tired. "We are groping in the dark, Phoemio. But we have no choice."

Chapter Thirteen

Several days later, Korax and Zeno tramped down the hill of Rhodos to keep an appointment with Staphylus. Leontes insisted on accompanying them, though they both would have preferred to spare the old man the excursion through the damp weather and the stresses of the meeting. Isochomachus stayed at home to try to comfort Callipatria.

Staphylus' office was located in a tree-lined arcade near the Assembly Hall and the Chambers of the Rhodian Council. A clerk ushered them through an outer room and into a well-appointed office. They sat down on a cushioned bench and faced Staphylus across a glossy ebony table. Behind his chair, a gilded lattice screen let in daylight, while keeping out the worst drafts.

"This really is a most unusual and intriguing case," Staphylus commented, studying a copy of the indictment as though it were a finely crafted vase.

"What is your opinion?" Zeno demanded gruffly.

Staphylus looked up, his face softening. "Forgive me if I sounded insensitive. I realize the uniqueness of the case holds no comfort for you gentlemen. The fact is, it's very hard to predict how this will play out. There has not been a trial for sorcery in Rhodos in ninety years—and there is none on record where the alleged losses are of such magnitude."

"What does the law say?" Zeno persisted. "Tell me the letter of the law."

Staphylus gave a brief grimace and waved at a set of scrolls on the table. "Regrettably, the law is vague. It says only that it is a crime to harm a citizen or damage his property through magic or witchcraft. It prescribes penalties 'commensurate with the gravity of the offence.' In this case, as Korax has surmised, that could mean fines, exile, or even execution."

Leontes gave a muted gasp, his countenance full of misery.

"Unfortunately," Staphylus went on, "as Zeno is named an accomplice, he would be liable to the same punishment as Korax, if the verdict is guilty."

Zeno shook his head, his lips pressed tight.

"What strategy do you advise?" Korax asked.

"Yes, quite so." With an air of professional competence, Staphylus referred to notes etched on wax tablet. "The case will be tried before Pythodoros. He is a just and reasonable magistrate, so we are fortunate there. A jury of 301 citizens will render the verdict. Since Amynias exercised his right to bring the charges on behalf of the Rhodians, he will plead the case and interrogate the witnesses. No doubt he has hired legal counsel to assist him, as you have done."

"Of course," Zeno growled. "A costly team of experts to aid him in his villainy."

"As for the specific charges, the first is that Korax bewitched Amynias into challenging him to wrestle. Though on its face this sounds ridiculous, you must remember what a bizarre act it was to provoke a wrestling match at a poetry salon. That point may carry some weight with the jury. Also, I have learned that Lyceas, and perhaps other of Amynias' friends, will give testimony. No doubt, they will claim to have seen some signs of magic or sorcery being done."

"They will be lying then," Korax asserted.

"Of course," Staphylus agreed. "But are there any witnesses you can rely on to dispute the story? Sadly, I myself was not present at the time."

"No one was there who is likely to take my side," Korax said. "Except Berenicea, of course."

Staphylus winced expressively. "Well, while calling a celebrated courtesan would increase the already spectacular notoriety of the case, I'm afraid her testimony wouldn't help us much. The typical juror will either be jealous that you have the affections of such a woman, or decide she's probably an enchantress herself."

"That is just as well," Korax responded. "I'd prefer to not involve her."

Staphylus nodded. "We'll rely on your own speech then. Hopefully, we can make Amynias appear as petty and ridiculous as he is. Now the second charge is that Korax used sorcery to protect the ships your family had interest in, and laid curses on competitors' vessels. This is by far the more serious allegation, as it involves harm to many citizens and huge financial losses. By implication, Amynias makes your sorcery responsible for all the economic woes of Rhodos. The charge seems to be based primarily on the testimony of this man Menas."

"A treacherous slave," Zeno declared. "No one should believe him."

"Exactly," Staphylus concurred. "The fact that Menas is a runaway slave definitely works to our advantage. Also, I have been able to confirm that Amynias is indeed harboring Menas. Again, this is to our benefit. I recommend that Zeno file a counterclaim against Amynias for stealing the slave. This will bolster our defense, that Amynias' charges are a malicious and criminal conspiracy. With your permission, Zeno, I will prepare the necessary documents and have them ready for you to sign by tomorrow."

"Very well, if you think it best," Zeno answered forlornly.

Staphylus marked a note on his tablet. "Now keep in mind that your other slaves can also be required to speak. The law even allows them to be tortured, if necessary, to compel their testimony.

So, if there is anything your slaves might say that will appear incriminating in any way, you must advise me now."

Korax shifted in his seat. Hesitantly, he described the contents of his chamber, the magical texts and implements, the map with the wax ships. As he spoke, Staphylus twisted his mouth with concern.

"It is true that I study occult philosophy," Korax concluded defensively. "And I did perform workings to safeguard our ships. But those are not crimes. I never laid curses on our fellow shippers. That allegation is a blatant lie."

"I believe you, of course," Staphylus said, scratching another note. "But we will need to consider how to present your activities in—shall we say?—the most positive light. I suggest I come to your house and view the room in question. Then we can work together on the oratory for your defense. Also, we can prepare the slaves how best to respond if they are called to testify. We have much work before us. Luckily, we have over a month till the trial date."

Korax nodded his assent.

"There is one more consideration," Staphylus added. "In reviewing the court documents, I learned that Korax does not have his citizenship. Although he was born in Rhodes, of a citizen family, he never completed his naval obligation."

"But that was not his fault," Leontes cried. "He was kidnapped and enslaved. He had no opportunity."

"Of course, I understand. I researched the matter and found that in such circumstances, a waiver can be granted. I suggest Korax apply for the waiver at once. It should be just a formality, but whether the citizenship is granted in time for the trial or not, the fact of the application will underscore that Korax is no foreigner, but a loyal son of Rhodes."

"Agreed," Korax said. "Will you prepare the petition for me, Staphylus?"

"Of course. I will send it round with the other documents tomorrow." He rose from his chair. "Are there any other questions or concerns I can answer for you, gentlemen?"

"Yes. What are our chances?" Leontes asked. "Please, sir, tell me the truth."

Staphylus circled the table and laid a hand on the old man's forearm. "As I told you, it is an unusual case. But I truly believe that your son Korax and I have two of the sharpest minds in Rhodos. Working together, I am confident we can carry the day."

But as Zeno led Leontes out of the office, Staphylus pulled Korax aside for a final word.

"I wanted to reassure your poor father, but I do not wish to leave you with too optimistic an impression. Amynias' charges are a concoction of falsehoods and innuendo. But given the troubled times we live in, and the superstitious nature of the populace, his case may look very appealing to a jury. Sadly, it is the nature of men to seek scapegoats, and Amynias has artfully positioned you for that role."

"I know the situation is grave," Korax said. "And I thank you for your diligence and expertise."

Staphylus leaned closer and whispered: "What I mean is, if you can work any magic charms that will help our cause, don't hesitate."

Recumbent in the broad, luxurious bed, Korax watched Berenicea dressing. She draped a long gown over her shapely body and tied the cords under her breasts. She paused to fluff out her gorgeous red hair.

"I'm sorry, my love. But I did mention I have another visitor calling this evening."

"I know." Korax smiled affectionately. "I have work to do at home anyway—although I would much prefer to linger in your arms all night."

He slipped out of bed and ambled naked across the carpet, searching for his garments. The shutters were drawn against the chill afternoon, so the fragrant chamber was only partially lit.

Berenicea sat at her dressing table, fixing combs in her hair. "I don't normally schedule two guests in one day. But this one is a navy man whose squadron has just landed. He's anxious to see me, as you can imagine. I actually hoped you might meet him downstairs. It would be good if the two of you talked."

Holding the chiton in front of his body, Korax frowned. "I gather you're referring to Patrollos."

"Please don't be angry with me, Korax. I am compelled by my belief that the hatred between you is unnecessary. I feel it is my duty to reconcile you."

"Given my current circumstances," Korax answered curtly, "reconciliation with Patrollos is not an urgent concern. He is a friend of Amynias, remember? For all I know, he will be testifying, telling lies against me at my trial."

"I'm sure he would never do that." Berenicea stood and regarded him with heartfelt dismay. "He regrets the harm he caused you in the past. Please do not be unkind to him."

Korax pulled the chiton over his head. "I hope to be gone before he arrives. But if I do meet him, I will not dishonor your hospitality. I promise to act with courtesy."

He finished dressing and walked downstairs with Berenicea. Patrollos was waiting in the entry room, wearing a pleated chiton under his gray navy cloak. He stood up from the couch and bowed abruptly when he recognized Korax.

"Patrollos." Korax tried to make polite conversation. "Welcome back to Rhodos. Will you stay ashore the rest of the season?"

During the winter, only a token force of squadrons patrolled the coast of Rhodes. Having just completed a tour, it was likely Patrollos would not sail again till spring.

"Yes. Forgive me, I did not realize the lady had other company."

"I was just leaving."

"Wait," Berenicea said. "I wish to speak with both of you. Will you walk with me in the garden? Please?"

She held out a hand to each of them. Korax and Patrollos eyed one another, then agreed reluctantly, compelled by her gentle appeal. The gatekeeper opened the garden doors and the three strolled the path together, Berenicea in the center, holding both of their hands. The overcast afternoon was beginning to fade into dusk.

At the rear of her garden was a fountain. In this season the water lay still and mossy, floating with dead leaves. On a pedestal in the center knelt a nude Aphrodite, gleaming white. The sculptor depicted the goddess at the moment of rising from her bed or bath. She lifted her thick tresses, tilted her head and smiled beguilingly as though at a lover.

Berenicea bowed her head before the fountain and prayed silently to her goddess. Korax and Patrollos stood to either side, shifting their feet.

Finally, Berenicea spoke in a soft, fervent voice. "Of all my men, you two are my favorites. It is childish, I know, but I think of you as my two heroes. Patrollos is my Achilles, fierce and strong, sullen and proud. Korax is my Odysseus, bold and clever and forced to be a wanderer. I love you both so much, I feel that you must be friends. But something malignant and evil prevents it. Korax believes Patrollos is to blame for more than a beating that happened long ago. Patrollos will not speak of his guilt, but I know it torments his soul. As a priestess, I urge you both: Patrollos, confess whatever it is. Korax, forgive whatever it is."

Patrollos shuddered, and might have walked off except that Berenicea still gripped his hand.

Korax waited. He certainly felt no obligation to speak first, before Patrollos confessed and begged forgiveness. But as the silence lengthened, Aphrodite's pervasive love seemed to dispel the bitterness in his heart.

"Patrollos, I have already forgiven you for our enmity in the past. And I have come to realize that Amynias is the author of much evil. Perhaps you were swept along in his current, even against your will. I do not need to know. You do not need to speak."

"You shame me," Patrollos gasped. "I always considered you less worthy than the rest of us, a half-blood. But you prove yourself more noble than me and the others by far. And that only deepens my dishonor."

He wrested his hand from the lady's hold. "Forgive me, Berenicea. I cannot stay."

"Wait," she cried. "Do not leave."

"I must. I cannot bear this."

Without looking at Korax, Patrollos spun and hastened away through the darkening courtyard.

From morning till night, Korax worked on his legal defense. He and Staphylus interviewed the slaves and tutored them in the best ways to present their testimony at the trial, should they be called. They wrote and rewrote speeches for Korax to deliver, trying to anticipate and answer all possible points. Korax committed the speeches to memory and practiced his delivery, while Staphylus listened critically and offered suggestions.

At night, Korax worked magic to shield the family from evil, and spent many hours peering into the scrying bowl. But no matter how hard he looked or how much blood he dripped into the water, the layers of cloud surrounding Amynias would not lift.

Then, six days before the trial, Phoemio burst into Korax's room. He was panting, having run all the way from the marketplace.

"Master, I have news about Amynias. I'm not sure it will be helpful, but it is news."

"Sit down, Phoemio. Catch your breath and tell me."

The slave collapsed onto a couch in the midst of the cluttered chamber. "I learned this from his cook, Stratola. I saw her at a coppersmith's stall, looking over pots and pans. She does not often come to the marketplace, so I took the chance to strike up a conversation. We talked about turnips and cabbages for a while and I flattered her cooking. Eventually, I worked around to asking when I might come by her kitchen door and beg a bowl of soup—thinking this would be a way to talk with the other slaves of the house. To my surprise, she told me to come tomorrow, as her master will be away for two days. She said he is riding upcountry to inspect his farmstead."

"That is strange," Korax muttered. "Only six days till the trial and Amynias wastes two of them on an excursion to the countryside."

"I thought it strange too," Phoemio said. "It must be an important matter."

Korax had not been able to learn much about Amynias' farm, except that it was located somewhere in the hills south of Rhodos. This time of year, it was hard to imagine what pressing business could take Amynias there.

Amynias must be feeling very sure of his case, Korax thought forlornly. Meantime his own confidence—what little there was—

had drained. Word of the trial had circulated through the town and people eyed Korax distrustfully wherever he went. Old acquaintances shunned him at the gymnasium, and people who recognized him in the street whispered behind his back and drew signs against the evil eye. Intuition told Korax he needed a fulcrum, a point of leverage to tip events in his favor—before their awful weight came crashing down.

"What will you do, master?" Phoemio asked.

"Follow him," Korax decided. "I will follow him into the country."

Chapter Fourteen

Early the next morning, Amynias left Rhodos on horseback through the Upland Gate. The road from that gate crossed a plateau south of the city, in the shadow of the town's acropolis, winding past the racetrack, vineyards and temple estates.

Perched on a hilltop above the road, Korax and Leukon sat on the backs of hired horses. Hidden among a stand of pine trees, they watched Amynias round a curve of the road within a hundred yards of their position. Amynias wore a brown chlamys and a wide-brimmed hat. He held the reins in one hand, his left arm concealed under his cloak. In the six months since the wrestling accident, it was known that his shoulder had never fully healed.

"Odd that he makes the journey alone," Korax said quietly. "No slave to accompany him on the road, especially with his injured arm."

"He rides like a man clutching secrets," Leukon observed. "But we will ferret them out."

The Celt's spirits were high, lifted by the open air and the prospect of adventure.

They watched Amynias ride past the Grove of Apollo, to the place where the road forked. One trail descended from the plateau and followed the coast to the nearby town of Ialysos. The other way, which Amynias chose, climbed into the highlands.

Korax counted to fifty, then kicked the flanks of his horse. He picked his way cautiously down the rugged hill, Leukon riding behind. They reached the road and started off at an easy pace.

All morning they followed the road as it wound through the hills, past farmsteads bordered by rough stone walls and planted with vineyards and orchards. Above them on the higher slopes, flocks of goats and sheep could sometimes be seen, speckling the rocky pastures. Occasionally, they rounded a turn and spotted Amynias ahead in the distance. Then they would drop back, lagging to let their quarry move farther ahead. Korax had spun a charm of concealment, but naturally it would be more reliable if they kept out of sight.

In the afternoon, rain showers drifted in from the sea. The rain muddied the road and made it easy for Leukon to track Amynias, so they were able to hang back at a safer distance. Amynias never stopped to rest, and by late afternoon Korax worried that his horses were straining. He and Leukon dismounted and walked them up a long, steep incline to a notch between two craggy peaks. They halted at the top of the ridge and stared down into a small, upland valley. Olive and pine trees clung to the slopes, while the bottom was a ragged patchwork of barren fields and neglected orchards.

"There." Leukon pointed to an old farmhouse built just off the road. Amynias had dismounted and was leading his horse into a ramshackle barn.

"He's stopping for the night," Korax said. "Let's find a spot where we can overlook him."

They pulled their mounts off the trail and clambered along the steep slopes near the rim of the valley. They chose a shelf above an outcropping, where they could view the farmhouse but still be hidden behind a line of trees. Korax sent Leukon off to tether the horses and find a spring or pool. He sat down behind the bole of a pine tree to keep watch.

Presently, he saw Amynias cross the courtyard and enter the house. The farm seemed deserted, and searching with his inner eye, Korax verified that it was so. This only deepened the enigma: Why should the citified banker own a disused farm in the hinterland? And why did he come here alone in the winter?

The daylight was fading when Leukon crept onto the outcropping to crouch behind Korax. He had watered and fed the horses and now placed a water skin and leather pouch on the ground. The two men ate a cold supper of dry bread and olives.

"It's a shame your cousin takes such poor care of his property," the Celt remarked, brooding over the valley. "He leaves his vineyards choked by weeds and his orchards unpicked and unpruned."

Korax chuckled mockingly. "Be careful, my friend. Kleis will make a farmer of you yet."

Leukon huffed. "If that happens, it will be your fault. A man must do something with his time. This is the first time in months you've had anything resembling warrior's work for me."

"And it might be the last," Korax said. "If I lose my case, you may end up owned by Amynias. What will you do then?"

Leukon grunted. "I swam the Nile once. Perhaps I can swim the straits between Rhodes and the mainland. Perhaps I will cut your cousin's throat for him before I—Ah, look!"

He pointed to a distant spot on the valley floor. His keen eyes had spied another traveler, a man leading a donkey. The man approached the farmhouse from the opposite way that Amynias had come. Peering into the twilight, Korax discerned a wiry figure in a tattered cloak. The donkey slumped under a heavy burden of sacks and parcels. The man looked like a peddler.

As he padded up to the house, the door opened. Amynias came out, carrying a lantern. The men exchanged a few words as they walked the donkey across the courtyard and into the barn.

"What now?" Leukon whispered. "Do we sneak down and listen to their talk?"

Korax considered the idea, but shook his head. "Too risky. Others might be coming."

The lantern flickered inside the barn for some time. Finally the men emerged and returned to the house. Amynias lit the way, and the peddler went after him, staggering under the weight of two heavy sacks. The farmhouse door shut, and the light was lost in the deep, pervasive blackness.

Korax and Leukon took turns standing watch, although in the starless night they could not even see the road. Neither of them heard anything from the direction of the farmhouse.

At dawn, Leukon shook Korax awake, and they slipped down the hill to their observation spot. Amynias and the peddler were moving in the courtyard. The peddler was arranging the load on his donkey as Amynias led the horse from the barn. A horse-cloth was already tied on the animal's back, but Amynias needed the help of the peddler to hoist two leather satchels and tie them in place. The bags looked heavy, and it appeared to Korax that the peddler's donkey now carried a much lighter burden.

Leukon noticed it also. "Your cousin takes some heavy stuff from the little man."

"Indeed, heavy like bags of coin," Korax murmured. An idea of what it all meant was starting to take shape.

As soon as the load was secured, Amynias spoke a few words to the other man then climbed onto the horse's back. He kicked the flanks and whipped the neck with his reins. The horse twisted its head and reluctantly started off. It ambled from the courtyard and headed up the trail toward Rhodos. Meantime, the peddler had grabbed his donkey's tether and marched off in the opposite direction.

"What next, Blackbird?" Leukon asked.

"We need to know what business passed between them, and I'm sure Amynias won't tell us. Let's have a talk with the other one."

By the time they readied their horses and found a safe path down the hillside, the peddler was nearly out of sight at the far end of the valley. But, trotting on horseback, they covered the ground quickly. They caught up with the man near the place where the road started rising into the hills.

The peddler heard them coming and looked around with a nervous start. He yanked his donkey to the side of the road to let the riders pass. The man looked older than Korax expected, with brown, weather-beaten skin. His close-set eyes watched them with hostile suspicion.

Korax and Leukon rode past him, then reined their mounts and jumped to the ground.

"Greetings, old father," Korax said, striding toward the man. "Where are you bound so early this morning?"

"I'm not your father, and my destination is none of your business." The man answered belligerently, but he flinched a bit as Korax and Leukon approached.

"But this is the road to Kamiros, is it not?"

"I suppose it is—Hey, what are you doing?"

Korax was examining the donkey's load, lifting sacks and pouches. The peddler seized his arm, but Leukon quickly restrained the man.

"Peace, little friend. My master means to have a look at your gear. He might want to buy something."

"Belay that! There's nothing for sale. There's nothing of value, I tell you."

Korax opened a satchel and found some sheets of papyrus.

"Leave that alone. I warn you, I have friends in Kamiros—dangerous men who will treat you roughly."

"Yes, I believe you," Korax said, scanning one of the documents. "Kamiros and other places too, I think. Let's take him back to the house so we can talk at leisure."

"No! Unhand me. Help! Help! Murderers!"

The old man's sinews were tough as knotty tree roots, and he put up a furious fight. But soon Leukon had him pinned to the ground with a knee at the small of his back. Korax lifted a chiton from the peddler's pack and tore it into strips. They used these to gag the man and bind his wrists and ankles. Leukon hoisted the wriggling, moaning prisoner over the back of one of their mounts. Taking the tethers of the donkey and horses, they hurried back to the farmhouse.

Korax and Leukon drew swords before pushing the door in, but as Korax expected the house was empty. They carried their prisoner inside and tossed him on the grimy floor. The house smelled of mold, with rotting planks in the floor and gaps in the thatch roof. Leukon opened the shutters, while Korax lit an oil lamp from embers that still smoldered in the hearth.

While Leukon kept watch outside, Korax sat down on a stool and examined the documents from the peddler's satchel. He found a ledger and a number of receipts. Amynias was not so careless as to use his own name and seal. Instead, he referred to himself throughout as "the Banker of Rhodes," and used a signet in the likeness of a ship's sail and sword. One name in the ledger caught Korax's eye. He sucked in his breath, deliberating over all the evidence.

He could see only one conclusion. And in that one dreadful answer, all the mysteries were solved: the rapid growth of Amynias' fortune, his extensive collecting of ships' manifests, even the failure of Korax's scrying. The business was hidden not to benefit Amynias, but his clients. And not by the workings of magic, but by the power of a god. Poseidon protected the sea-wolves of Crete, and Amynias was in league with them.

Korax loosened the gag from the old man's jaws.

"Let me go," the man panted. "You have no right to waylay a poor traveler."

"You're not so poor as you pretend," Korax answered in a soft, menacing voice. "How much silver did you carry to this house last night? Close to 8,000 drachmas, according to the receipts. I know you're just a courier, but I'm sure you take a suitable cut."

The man clenched his lips, glaring.

"I also know whose money it is. I recognize one of the names, a certain Olbius whom I remember very well. I spent some months as his hostage in Crete."

"I warn you! You'd better let me go."

Korax brought the lamp close to the man's head and scrutinized an old scarring of the earlobe. "Yes, a triple piercing in the left ear. I've seen this mark before, my friend. You sailed with the pirates in your day."

"If you know that, then you know I'll never talk. No threats or torture will untie my tongue."

"Perhaps we'll test that before the day is through. I need to know how long Amynias—your banker—has been in partnership with the Cretans. And aside from investing their money, what other services does he provide them? Does he apprise them of cargos and shipping schedules, for example?"

The man clamped his mouth and twisted his face away.

Korax sighed. To have any hope of exposing Amynias, he would need not only this man's confession, but his testimony in Rhodos. He went outside to talk with Leukon. They discussed the situation and finally agreed on a plan. They found some rope and iron tools in the barn. They carried these into the house and dropped them noisily on the floor in front of their prisoner. While Leukon held the man immobile, Korax untied and stripped him naked. They tossed the rope over a rafter and strung up the man by his ankles.

"Torture will do you no good," the man gasped fearfully. "I will never talk."

Korax grabbed the man's skull and forced him to look at the hearth. Leukon had set down the iron tools and was stoking the fire.

"You might want to reconsider your position," Korax said. "My henchman is a barbarian of the north. In the gloomy forests of his homeland, they have devised tortures no civilized man ever dreamed of."

He released the man and let him swing from the creaking beam. Leukon hummed to himself as he heated the iron tools in the fire: a scythe, rusty shears, a poker. The hanging man kept turning his head to watch. Gradually, his look of grim resolve melted.

When the shears glowed red, Leukon carried them over and showed them to his victim. The Celt smiled with evil anticipation.

"Will you start with the eyes or the genitals?" Korax inquired.

"The man-parts first, I think," Leukon said contemplatively. "That will cause agony without immediately threatening his life. I remember one Illyrian prisoner. We roasted his balls while they were still attached to him. By the time he talked, the place smelled like goose on a spit."

Korax nodded, hiding a smile. At first reluctant to playact the role of torturer, Leukon was now performing with imaginative flair.

"I will wait outside," Korax informed their victim. "I lack the stomach for watching. My name is Korax. If you change your mind and are ready to talk, call me. Be sure you call loudly though. Once he starts his fiendish work, it is very hard to make him stop."

Halfway across the floor he heard the man cry out. "Wait! Don't leave me with this savage. I will talk!"

Korax swung and waved Leukon back.

"Only promise me a merciful death," the captive pleaded. "Let me be put to the sword or given the hemlock to drink, not pegged up on your city walls."

"Your fate will be up to the Rhodian Council," Korax answered. "But if you help me expose the traitor Amynias, I believe they will show mercy. They might even spare your life and give you a stipend as a friend of the city."

"Then I am your man. I will tell you everything, only let me down first."

"No, first I want to hear your story. You can begin by telling me your name."

"Very well. It is Bolocrates."

Chapter Fifteen

In all Rhodos, the Temple of Athene was second in grandeur only to that of Helios. It faced the harbor, not far from the Square of the Colossus, with glistening pillars of white Attic marble and painted friezes above the colonnades.

On the noon before the day of his trial, Korax went to the temple alone. He burned incense on the steps and laid a wreath of olive branches in the portico. Then he walked inside to pray. Athene's statue stood armed with buckler and spear, but the visage under her silver helmet was mild.

"Bright-eyed Athene," Korax whispered. "Daughter of Zeus and defender of cities, accept the offerings of a Rhodian who is bound to you in honor and duty."

"I am here for you, man of Rhodes." The voice sounded clearly in his head.

"I ask your special intervention at my trial."

"You know I am already on your side. You fear you will not win the case."

"It is true."

He and Leukon had returned to Rhodos with Bolocrates and now had the man locked in a storeroom at Zeno's house. Staphylus had listened with astonishment to the old pirate's story, and had labored for three days to recast their entire defense around it. Staphylus seemed to believe they now had a real chance of turning the tables on Amynias. Still, Korax was tormented by doubt.

"I have a pirate's agent as a witness, and some documents I cannot even prove were penned by Amynias. He has the testimony of Menas and Lyceas, and the fear and prejudice of the city on his side. He is a respected banker and friend to the ruling families, while I am viewed as a half-Thracian mongrel, not even a citizen."

"You forget one thing," Athene told him. "You have justice on your side."

"That is true, goddess. Yet I have seen enough of this world to know that justice does not always prevail."

The day of the trial dawned chilly and bright. From early morning, the square in front of the Assembly Hall was mobbed with people hoping to secure a seat inside.

For the last month, the trial had been anticipated and gossiped about all over town, from the docks and arcades of the Emporium to the gymnasia, the barbershops, and the stalls of the marketplace. The case had a fabulous mixture of ingredients to captivate an idle populace in the dull months of winter: allegations of witchcraft, a traitorous runaway slave, witnesses from the ruling families, a brawl at the house of a celebrated hetaera. Satirists and scandalmongers found incomparable material for their arts. Was the shadowy son of Leontes a dangerous sorcerer? Or had the crafty moneylender Amynias concocted the whole scheme in bitter revenge for the crippling of his arm? The most outrageous tales were sworn to as known facts: Korax had mastered the magic of Egypt and succeeded in levitating the pyramids; he had seduced Queen Arsinoe with enchantments, inciting King Ptolemy to murder her in a jealous rage. It was even claimed Korax had been killed once by Amynias, but that his witch mother raised him from the dead.

The bronze doors of the Assembly Hall opened and the crowd surged forward, all but overwhelming the bailiffs who brandished their truncheons and bawled for order. When all the seats within were taken, a straggling mob lingered in the square and along the colonnades. Their steady murmur rose in volume when the magistrate Pythodoros appeared, leading the 301 jurors chosen by lot to decide the case.

A little later, some in the crowd cheered when Amynias arrived, flanked by his three lawyers, supposedly the most learned and clever barristers in Rhodes. Behind Amynias walked his friend and partner Lyceas and a small, greedy-eyed slave that everyone took to be Menas, the star witness. The more well-informed spectators also pointed out Amynias' garishly-attired mother, Epiteleia, strutting along with her other son Hegestratus, a sullen and brawny ship's captain.

Despite the rising excitement, the entire square grew hushed a while later when Korax arrived. The accused sorcerer walked with a satchel under his arm and a look of bleak resolve etched on his thin, dark face. With him came his uncle and supposed accomplice, the stout old merchant Zeno, and his legal advisor Staphylus, himself the son of a ruling family. A step behind them, a slave guided Korax's unfortunate father, the quivering, half-blind Leontes. Beside them walked Isochomachus, Zeno's nephew and partner in the family business. And in the rear of the party marched Korax's infamous slave, the huge, fearsome barbarian. Some claimed he was an exiled Celtic king, while others said his mother was a giantess. The grim Celt kept a firm grip on the arm of another man, a brown and weathered old sailor whom no one seemed to recognize.

As he mounted the steps, Korax gazed at the carvings above the high, open doorway. For some reason, the moment reminded him of his initiation, long ago, in the underground vault of the House of Life in Egypt. Only now there was no Amasis, no wise and benevolent master, to guide him through the trials.

Korax posted Leukon to wait with Bolocrates just inside the door. He did not want Amynias or anyone else to see the pirate's agent until the proper moment.

The interior of the Assembly Hall, a square with four banks of tiered seats, was jammed with hundreds of spectators. Above the seats crowded galleries stood before tall colonnades open to the daylight. On the floor, a gold and blue mosaic depicted the Colossus of Helios.

Korax and his party followed a bailiff to their assigned seats on one of the bottom rows. Across from them sat Amynias with his witnesses and lawyers. Korax noticed with dismay that many members of the ruling families occupied the rows behind Amynias. He spotted Patrollos with his father and brother, Lyceas and his family, officers of the navy and officials of the town. This arrangement could hardly be an accident.

A man with a herald's wand strode across the floor and waved his arms for quiet. He struck his wand on the floor three times and announced the presence in the hall of the magistrate Pythodoros. The magistrate rose from his place in front of the jury. Clad in a robe of scarlet and gold, he unfurled a papyrus and spoke in oratorical tones that resounded through the chamber.

"Under the aegis of Helios, Zeus, and Athene, and in the name of the citizens of Rhodes, I call this court to order. Amynias, son of Callias, on behalf of the Rhodians, charges Korax, son of Leontes, with doing him personal injury, and doing harm to the citizens of Rhodes, their property and treasure, by sorcery and witchcraft. Zeno, son of Autolycus, is further charged as a culpable accomplice. Let it be recorded that the jury is counted and present and both the complainant and defendants are in the hall. I now call on Amynias to present his case."

Head bowed solemnly, Amynias walked to the center of the floor. In a powerful voice, he summarized the points of his indictment. While he spoke he gestured with his right hand, keeping the other arm concealed beneath his draped himation.

The slaves of Zeno's house had received no summons, so Korax knew they would not be called to testify after all. Instead, Amynias' first witness was his clerk Hicesius. The slim, bearded Etruscan recounted how he had served Leontes in former days. He testified that it was well known in the house that Leontes' Thracian wife, Korax's mother, practiced witchcraft. More, the merchant often discussed the shipping business with his wife in private, which everyone considered most eccentric and bizarre. And it was no secret that, while Anticleia lived, the business prospered, the family's wealth growing in magnitude well beyond that of rival shippers.

While the Etruscan spoke, Korax glanced at his father. Leontes' listened with consternation, blinking to hold back his tears.

Next, Amynias introduced Menas. In doing so, he admitted to harboring the runaway slave who fled to his house for protection. Amynias excused this breach of the law on the grounds that shielding the witness and bringing his testimony before the court was a necessity to serve the higher good.

Menas, a hunched, gray-haired man, spoke in a timid and querulous voice. The magistrate had to admonish him several times to speak louder. He recounted how the family's business had improved soon after Korax arrived home from Egypt. He described the state of Korax's chamber, full of braziers and weird implements, books etched with arcane symbols, and a map with tiny ships carved of wax. He claimed to have heard Korax late in the night, torturing blood sacrifices and shrieking as he called down curses on rival merchants.

"Liar," Zeno grumbled. "Treacherous knave."

"His lies will doom us," Phoemio whispered, outraged. "What can we do?"

"Be still, please," Staphylus warned. "We will have our chance to respond."

The jury and spectators listened in rapt attention to Menas, and when he finished a restless muttering spread through the hall. Pythodoros waved his arms and demanded silence.

Lyceas was called next. He testified about the poetry salon, where he claimed to have observed Korax off in a corner, dropping a pinch of powder into a brazier and mumbling. Moments later, a pall came over Amynias. Speaking like a man in a dream, he challenged Korax to wrestle.

Korax could only shake his head at the unabashed falsehood of the tale. Lyceas, tense and perspiring, finished his account and slouched back to his seat. Amynias strode before the jury to present his summation.

"My friends and fellow citizens, you have heard the condemnation of witnesses: That Korax is the son of a witch, a Thracian crone who long ago conspired in secret with her husband to enrich themselves at the expense of others. That Korax himself, after learning magic in Egypt, came back to Rhodes in the past year and immediately resumed his mother's pernicious practices. And you have heard Lyceas, a nobleman and respected banker, testify that Korax worked a magic charm to incite me into challenging him.

"Those who know me know that, whatever my faults, I am a gentleman and would never act so crudely had my mind been not enthralled. Perhaps, because I suspected his sorcery, Korax bore me malice. But with cunning deceit, he bewitched *me* into challenging *him*, so that he might appear blameless. You have heard the true account, but you have not yet seen the result."

Amynias pulled aside his garment to show his crippled arm. The men of the jury grimaced, cringed, and hissed air through their teeth. The arm was sallow and withered, like a dying branch.

Amynias demonstrated how he could not close the fingers and could barely turn the wrist.

"It has lost its strength and will likely never heal. But I do not expose this shameful weakness to complain of my affliction. Nor would I have brought the charges against Korax if this was his only offense. No, I reveal my crippled arm to impress upon you the damage that Korax is capable of.

"By far his greater crime is what he has done to the merchants and citizens of Rhodos—the cursing of their voyages and ships. We all know how many vessels were lost this past season to storms, how many cargoes stolen by pirates. Now, clearly, you know the cause of these misfortunes.

"As for Zeno, he is my uncle and it grieves me sorely to involve him in this case. His only crime is harboring Korax in his house. Perhaps he did not even know the evils Korax performed under his roof—though I admit that seems unlikely. But Zeno is an old man and might easily have been fooled. For him, I ask your clemency."

"Old man," Zeno whispered under his breath. "Oh, for an hour alone with Amynias and a rod."

"But as for Korax," Amynias went on, "though he is my cousin and kinsman, and it makes me heartsick to denounce him, I cannot avoid it. His witchcraft is like a scorpion in our beds, an infection in our bodies that must be expelled. I charge you, men of Rhodes, to convict Korax of his crimes and sentence him to death."

Amynias let his words linger in the air as he stared into the faces of the jurors. He turned in the silent hall and walked slowly back to his seat.

Murmuring started again, but now it was low and somber. Pythodoros soon quelled the noise and called on Korax to present his defense.

Staphylus leaned over and patted his hand. "Justice is with you, my friend."

On watery legs, Korax trod to the center of the quiet chamber. Inwardly he whispered prayers to Athene and Helios.

"People of Rhodes, I tell you in plain honesty that the charges against me are false. I will answer them one by one and tell you the truth.

"First, it is true my mother was of Thrace and followed the sacred ways of her people. But she lived in Rhodos many years as a dutiful wife and is buried with my father's kin. She never harmed anyone by word or deed—to say otherwise is an evil lie. Yes, my father's business prospered in those years, but so did many others. The prosperity came from the grace of the gods and the hard work of my father and uncle. They earned wealth in partnership with many of you, merchants, bankers, and tradesmen of Rhodos, who shared in their good fortune.

"Secondly, it is true I lived among the Egyptians and studied their Mysteries. I read much philosophy that is foreign and obscure—but this is no crime. In Rhodes we are free men; the inscription on our Colossus celebrates the unfettered freedom we enjoy by the generosity of the gods and the valor of our fathers. Surely this must include freedom of thought and belief as well as action, so long as no one is harmed. And I have harmed no one.

"I dispute the testimony of Lyceas. He could not have seen me whisper magic words or drop powder in a brazier, because it never happened. Lyceas is scion of a noble family, but I believe he has been seduced into uttering these falsehoods by Amynias, his friend and partner. I wrestled Amynias only after he challenged me, out of his own malice. I regret the crippling of his arm, but I defended myself, as is any man's right.

"Now we come to the most serious charge, that I cursed the shippers of Rhodes and caused them disasters. When we examine the troubles in our sea trade, we find two main causes: bad weather and piracy. I make no claims on the weather; it is the province of the gods alone. But as to the devastation caused by pirates, while preparing my defense I discovered the man who is truly to blame. It is the very same Amynias who seeks to mask his crimes by indicting me."

A clamor swept up the tiered seats at this accusation.

"Outrageous," someone cried. "He lies."

"It is true," Korax shouted. "Amynias has conspired against Rhodes and aided the pirates of Crete. For years he has passed them information about our shipping, and enriched himself by banking their stolen silver." He waved papyrus sheets handed to him by Staphylus. "I have the evidence here, receipts written in his own hand. And I have a witness to prove the charges. Bring in Bolocrates of Kamiros."

The hall fell silent as Bolocrates shuffled across the mosaic floor. Korax observed a visage of blank shock on Amynias, and spied similar expressions on Patrollos and Lyceas. Bolocrates stopped beside Korax and eyed the vast audience with a cringing apprehension.

"Tell the truth loud and plain," Korax warned him. "Remember, it is your best hope to avoid execution."

Once he began, Bolocrates seemed almost eager. He had come to despise Amynias and, now that it served his self-interest, welcomed the chance to bring the banker down. He confessed he made his living as a friend of the pirates, carrying messages and conveying ransoms. He explained how, for the past three years, he had passed information from Amynias, detailing the cargoes and courses of freighters sailing from Rhodes. Further, he transported coin from the pirates, which he understood Amynias invested in Rhodos and in other banks overseas.

"This is fantastic beyond belief," Amynias shouted in the hushed hall. "What is there to suggest I've even met this man?"

"Amynias, you are out of order," the magistrate called.

"It is answered," Korax cried. "Bolocrates, tell the court how you first came to know Amynias."

"Oh, that was years ago. I came to Rhodos to arrange the ransom of a hostage held in Crete. It was this same Korax, the son of Leontes. But after Leontes paid me, I had a visit from Amynias and some other young men. For reasons they would not tell, they paid me extra coin to ensure Korax would not be set free."

A new uproar rose, a confused and chaotic melee of voices.

"Lies!" Amynias bellowed above the din. "This man is a confessed brigand and obvious perjurer. This is more of Korax's trickery. He seeks to deflect the charges onto an honest man."

"No! It is Amynias who lies. Bolocrates is telling the truth!"

In stunned silence, everyone stared at the speaker, who had bolted up from his seat among the ruling families. It was Patrollos.

"I know Bolocrates speaks the truth," he said, more hesitantly. "Because I was one of the men who paid him."

Chapter Sixteen

Silence gripped the Assembly Hall, a shocked and profound quiet. Korax stood in the center of the eerie scene, glancing at Patrollos, Amynias, Staphylus, not knowing what to do next.

Finally Pythodoros took charge. "Patrollos of the House of Philophron, if you have testimony for the court, come forward and speak."

Grimly, Patrollos descended from his place and marched over to face the jury. In a voice taut and ragged, but strong enough for all to hear, he confessed how he had beaten Korax on the street, then conspired with Amynias to pay off Bolocrates.

"I feared Korax would return to Rhodes and dishonor me," he said. "Instead, I dishonored myself. I kept the secret all these years rather than bring shame on my family. But I knew nothing of Amynias' later dealings with Bolocrates. I never suspected his crimes and treachery against Rhodes. Hearing Bolocrates disclose them today, I could no longer keep silent."

Bowing his head, Patrollos walked slowly back to his seat. As he climbed the steps, Lyceas jumped up in the hushed chamber.

"My lord magistrate, I too have evidence to give—I mean, more testimony."

"Come forward and speak, Lyceas," Pythodoros told him.

Refusing to look at Amynias, Lyceas hurried over toward the jury. First, he confessed that he too had been involved in the meeting with Bolocrates and with plotting to prevent Korax's release. Then he recanted his earlier testimony, admitting that he lied, under pressure from Amynias, in stating that he had seen Korax cast a spell prior to the wrestling match. Finally, he told the jury that he believed Bolocrates' charges, because they explained a number of large sums of silver that Amynias had deposited in the bank over the years, for which he never made adequate accounting.

Lyceas did not return to his seat. Instead he avoided going near Amynias and walked quickly out of the hall. Amynias himself sat very still, shoulders hunched, eyes darting wildly—like a man watching his house slowly collapse around him.

"We have heard some extraordinary testimony," Pythodoros said, "all of it certainly relevant to the case. But Korax was interrupted in the midst of his defense. Do you have further evidence to present, sir?"

Korax shook off his daze. "Only the summation, Lord Magistrate." He walked toward the jury, collecting his wits. "I thank Patrollos and Lyceas both for coming forward and speaking the truth under most difficult circumstances. With their help, the real traitor to Rhodes has been revealed. I suggest that Amynias be arrested and charged with treason. I plead clemency for Bolocrates, who has served our city as an informer. He is ready to give the names of his accomplices in Kamiros, so I recommend a galley be dispatched there at once to arrest those men. Finally, I repeat that I am innocent of ever harming anyone in Rhodes through sorcery, and I ask the jury to acquit me and my uncle of these false charges. This concludes my defense."

As Korax paced across the floor, someone from among the ruling families shouted "Bravo!" By the time he reached his seat, the entire hall was filled with applause and roars of acclamation.

When the ballots were counted, Korax and Zeno were overwhelmingly acquitted. After announcing the verdict, Pythodoros ordered Amynias arrested for treason and Bolocrates taken into custody as a witness. The magistrate told Korax that he too would be required to testify at Amynias' trial. But for now he was free to go, "with the thanks of the Rhodians."

While the island's constitution provided for an Assembly of citizens and a degree of democracy, the true power of the state remained with the nobility. Through their Council and appointed Archons, the so-called "ruling families" controlled finances, diplomacy, and the military. This arrangement was generally deemed proper, since the aristocracy had built the navy and established Rhodes as a free state with its capital at Rhodos. Through various levies and liturgies, they paid a predominant share of state expenses.

Because Amynias was charged with treason, his trial fell under the jurisdiction of the Council. Five days after his own trial, Korax testified before a tribunal of nine judges, all from the ruling families. The tribunal convened in an auditorium of the Council Chambers, similar in design to the Assembly Hall but much smaller. Along with the judges and scribes, only a few spectators were present, all members of the nobility.

Korax recounted what he had discovered on following Amynias into the country, and presented the ledger and receipts he had taken from Bolocrates. He answered a few questions from the judges and repeated his request that Bolocrates be granted clemency. All the time, Amynias sat watching him with a mien of aloof disinterest, like a man playing draughts for very low stakes. His lack of emotion sent a chill through Korax's blood.

The lead judge thanked Korax for his testimony and dismissed him. He did not learn the outcome of the trial till the following day, when Staphylus paid him a visit. As a noble and son of a magistrate, Staphylus was privy to the tribunal and had attended the entire proceeding. He showed up at Zeno's gate with a satchel under his arm and a sly, mysterious smile.

"Your cousin's fate is decided," Staphylus remarked, taking a seat on a bench in Zeno's garden. "He is exiled, stripped of citizenship, and all his property is forfeit. But he does escape with his life."

"Really?" Korax stood, one foot resting on the edge of the bench. "I admit I am surprised at that."

"You should be outraged. They were ready enough to hang you up in irons, believe me. But Amynias had a few markers left to play."

"What do you mean?"

"Banks in Cos and Caria where he deposited some of the pirates' funds. He agreed to turn those accounts over to the treasury—though I suspect what he returns will be only a small part of what he has secreted away."

"I don't care," Korax decided. "So long as he leaves Rhodes and never comes back."

"There are many who feel that way," Staphylus replied with a cynical laugh. "You see, that's the other reason he escaped the executioner. Quite a few of our leading citizens made money with Amynias, not just Lyceas and his father. Amynias claimed to have documents implicating many important men. Of course, it's doubtful any of them knew he was in partnership with the brigands. Still, such disclosures would stir up considerable resentment, especially among the merchants and seafarers who lost so much to piracy."

"Those same men will resent Amynias' escaping execution," Korax pointed out. "They will smell what is being concealed."

"Well, that brings us to the good news." Staphylus brightened. "The tribunal decreed that the property seized from Amynias will be used to pay restitution to all citizens who have suffered losses to the pirates. I am sure that will mollify much resentment."

"That will help my family," Korax said. "What happens to Bolocrates?"

"Oh, he made out even better than Amynias. He got his freedom and a reward of five hundred drachmas for informing against his fellow rogues. The tribunal was in a generous mood—which reminds me, the best news of all and the main reason I came to see you."

Standing, he reached into his satchel and produced a sealed papyrus. "When a man is convicted of crimes against the state and forfeits his property, the law bestows one-fifth of the property on the citizen who brought the charges. As your legal representative, I thought it incumbent on me to remind the tribunal of this point and that you were the one who brought Amynias' crimes to light."

"That's true. But legally, I am not a citizen."

"Remarkably enough, one of the judges had the churlishness to point that out. I swiftly answered that we have duly filed a petition to restore your citizenship, and I argued how unjust it would be to deny you your legal right—unjust and unpopular, since you are quite a hero right now. Your name is all over the town: 'Korax, the wily magician,' 'the conjurer of Rhodes.'" He pulled out a second papyrus. "Here's your approved petition; you are now officially a full citizen. This other document is your title to one-fifth of Amynias' property. Of course, the accounting has only just begun. But when it's over, you are going to be quite a wealthy fellow, I'm sure."

Korax gazed at the two rolls in his hand and grinned with amazement. "Staphylus, you are truly a valuable friend."

Staphylus gave a flippant bow. "Thank you for saying so. And please communicate that fact to your uncle. I'd like him to know that not *all* lawyers are despicable knaves."

"I for one am happy to be leaving Rhodes," Epiteleia announced, poking at a piece of radish. "I've never really felt at home here, since your dear father died."

The family occupied their separate couches in the dim dining room of her house. Epiteleia in her flashing jewelry stared unhappily at her tuna and vegetables. Hegestratus, in a rough sailor's chiton, was already deep into his third cup of wine. Amynias sat on the edge of his couch, unable to recline comfortably due to his fragile shoulder.

"I'll be much happier among my own people in Halicarnassus," Epiteleia continued. "I think we all will. Still, Amynias, all your property seized! I can't believe it. It is so unfair."

"I wish you would stop repeating that sentiment, mother. It does no good to complain." Amynias spoke without parting his teeth. The worst aspect of losing his house was being forced to lodge temporarily with his insufferable family. It was only the second day and already his mother's prattle was driving him mad.

"Yes, stop your caterwauling," Hegestratus growled. "There's nothing unfair about it. My little brother is a treacherous dog. He's lucky they didn't hang him on the city walls for the crows to pick."

"Not lucky," Amynias answered icily. "Clever."

"Oh, you are so clever," his brother sneered. "So sneaky and shrewd. You've lost everything! I'm surprised they left you a cloak to cover your scrawny backside."

Amynias eyed him contemptuously, then stood. "I've had enough to eat and too much of this vulgar company."

"That's right, scuttle away," Hegestratus made an obscene gesture. "Get out of my sight, little dog."

"Don't leave," Epiteleia cried. "Can't we all get along as a family for once? How will we ever manage in Halicarnassus?"

"You don't have to come with me," Amynias shouted. "I was exiled, not you. I'd prefer it if you both stayed in Rhodes."

"And you think that's even possible," his mother demanded, "with the shame you've brought on us? None of my friends will even speak to me. Loutish commoners curse me in the streets. Oh, that I had never lived to suffer such indignities! I thank Hecate your poor father died long ago, for this disgrace would certainly have killed him!"

Amynias was out the door and up the stairs, Epiteleia's yowls fading in his ears. He would have to endure their company for at least another six days: three days till the specially commissioned Rhodian trireme carried them into exile, another three before it reached Halicarnassus. Sailing this time of year was a rarity under any circumstances, but Caria was just across the straits and up the coast, and the Council had deemed it prudent for Amynias to depart with all possible haste.

He reached his bedroom and slammed the door, enraged. He planned to be free of his irksome mother and brother as soon as he landed in Halicarnassus. Amynias had money hidden there, and contacts to arrange for his transport out of the city.

His forearm burned with a dull, bloated pain. Cursing, he stripped the chiton off his chest and cut away the bandages with a knife. The arm had swollen again, the skin a grayish purple. The physicians advised against bleeding the arm too often, but Amynias did not care. He considered them all fools, their healing arts useless.

He sat down and placed the arm over a wide bowl. With courage fueled by his rage, he calmly sliced his flesh. He watched with a dull, aloof expression as the blood trickled out and dripped into the bowl.

His brother was wrong: he had not lost everything. He still had his nerve and his instincts. Already these qualities were helping him birth a new plan. He still had allies in Crete, and they had grown more powerful than the Rhodians suspected. The Fates had driven Amynias down, crippled him, robbed him of his wealth and property, but they had not defeated him, not yet. Someday, he would come back to Rhodes and settle accounts with all his enemies.

Chapter Seventeen

Everyone in Zeno's house was surprised at the invitation. The entire family was asked to a banquet at the House of Philophron. While in the past Zeno and Leontes had often done business with men of the ruling families, they had never been invited to mix with them socially. For days preceding the event, Zeno and Leontes discussed the matter with curious anticipation, while Callipatria fussed over what gown to wear and how she ought to style her hair.

The family arrived at the manor gates in late afternoon. Zeno, Callipatria, and Isochomachus all looked stiff and anxious in their carefully draped himations. Leontes, freshly shaved and perfumed, walked haltingly on Phoemio's arm. Only Korax appeared at ease. For a man who had lived in the Temple of Ptah and dined at the palace of the Ptolemies, the house of a Rhodian noble held no special awe.

Still, he felt curious and a little wary.

These feelings sharpened when the family was ushered into a pillared dining room overlooking the garden. Forty or fifty couches had been laid. The chamber was crowded with members of the ruling families.

Halitherses, the slim and gracious lord of the house, stepped forward personally to greet Zeno and his party. "Gentlemen, lady, I am so happy to welcome you."

"My lord, you honor us." Zeno clasped his wrist.

"On the contrary, it is you who do us the honor. Come."

Halitherses conducted the family through the hall, introducing them to many of his aristocratic guests. Korax exchanged formal courtesies with Cimon and Lyceas, with the magistrate Pythodoros and the city Archon, Cleisthenes. He was delighted to meet Staphylus, who smiled ironically and winked.

Halitherses led the family to couches reserved for them on the dais. He introduced his wife, Choronice, his sons Patrollos and Agesilaus, and his daughter, the golden-haired Thalia.

Patrollos stood solemnly and welcomed the guests to his father's house. Korax sensed the man's humiliation. He reflected on how painful it must have been for Patrollos to confess his guilt in the Assembly Hall. He wanted to express his gratitude, but this was too public a place.

Dinner commenced to a lilting tune of flutes. Servants carried in silver kraters, trays, and platters. The fare was plain but abundant—Rhodian wine, seafood with briny sauces, olives, fruits, and bread.

While the guests dined, Halitherses made it a point to converse with Korax and his family. He extolled Korax's speech at the trial, his discernment and valor in exposing Amynias' crimes. He expressed satisfaction that the family would receive recompense for their financial losses over the years, in addition to the part of Amynias' fortune that the tribunal had awarded to Korax.

"It is true, we have had quite a windfall," Zeno remarked. "Now we can pay off our debts and hopefully keep our business on a prosperous course."

"With Amynias no longer passing information to the pirates," Leontes said, "the chances are good for all the shippers of Rhodes to prosper again."

"Let us pray to the gods that it be so," Halitherses agreed. "But your family in particular has suffered much hardship. I trust you feel that Korax's reward is adequate, that justice has been served?"

This was the surreptitious purpose of the banquet, Korax realized. Halitherses wanted assurance that Korax had forgiven the past, that he would not seek damages against Patrollos and the others for betraying him into slavery. He glanced over at Patrollos, who listened with eyes downcast.

"I assure you, my lord," Korax said to Halitherses, "I am satisfied with the reward and more than happy to put the bitterness of the past behind me."

"That is nobly said," his host answered. "I am acutely aware of the crimes committed against you, and the part played by my own son. His dishonor is a stain on the House of Philophron that will not diminish."

Patrollos quivered at these words, but remained stoically silent.

Korax's empathy was like a twinge in the gut. "I must disagree, my lord," he said. "When Patrollos spoke out at my trial, he saved me and my family from disaster, and he rescued Rhodes from the clutches of Amynias. It cost him dearly to make that confession in front of the whole town, but that did not stop him. Certainly, this courageous act of self-sacrifice restored his honor and that of your family."

Halitherses stood, eyes moist, and bowed to Korax. "You are generous to say so, my friend. Rhodes is fortunate to count you among her citizens, and your father is fortunate indeed to have so noble a son."

Korax looked around, a bit embarrassed. Choronice and Thalia stared at him, plainly moved. Zeno, Leontes, and Callipatria all beamed proudly. Patrollos continued to avoid his eyes.

After dinner, many of the guests stepped out to the terrace and gardens, where lanterns gleamed in the cool twilight. Korax took the opportunity to wander off by himself. The overwrought emotions at dinner left him wanting a little solitude.

But as he strolled between the slim cypresses and the reflecting pool, a small woman approached him. It was Patrollos' sister Thalia, wrapped in a purple shawl, her hair hanging loose around her shoulders.

"Please pardon my following you. I only wanted to thank you for what you said about Patrollos. My father has been very hard on him."

"I hope I have dispelled your father's concerns," Korax answered. "There is no further need for any of us to be troubled about the past."

Her eyes sparkled in the lamplight. They were a gray color, Korax thought.

"I am told you've studied much philosophy. Is that what makes you so compassionate?"

He smiled at the compliment. "I suppose it has forced me to face my own flaws, and that tends to make you more forgiving of others."

"I see." They started to stroll in step. "I also owe you a debt of gratitude, you know. I was betrothed to Amynias. But for you, I would have married a traitor to Rhodes. Imagine how that would have disgraced the House of Philophron."

"Amynias deceived many people. There is no disgrace in having been gulled by him."

"Still, I seem fated to be most unlucky in the picking of husbands. Do you believe in fate, master philosopher?"

"Oh, yes. But not as an absolute."

"And what does that mean?"

Korax considered his reply. "I think certain events are fated. But how we choose to respond to them—that determines their effect on us, and influences what comes after. So, in a way, we forge our own fates."

Thalia twisted her mouth. "Your philosophy offers me small comfort. If I have made my own fate, I have done it poorly."

"You will find a husband," Korax assured her. "With your beauty and your family name, you have much to recommend you."

"Oh, thank you for saying so," she laughed faintly. "It seems to be your evening for showing kindness to my family. But look, here is my brother."

They had wandered back to the terrace. Patrollos strode toward them and bowed to Korax.

"I must thank you for what you said to my father. Once again, I am in your debt."

"There is no debt, Patrollos. You repaid all at my trial. I tried to make that clear."

"My father is correct that you are most noble," Patrollos said. "I wish we could be friends."

"Why can't you be?" Thalia demanded.

"Do *you* not understand?" Patrollos inquired of Korax. "Every time I lay eyes on you, I see my own shame and dishonor. I can never forget it or live it down. Nor will my father ever forgive me. Even today, when you sought to reconcile us, it only prompted him to say how proud he would be to have *you* for a son."

"Your father will forget in time," Korax said.

"No, you do not know him. You do not appreciate the disgrace I brought on the family. I am glad there is peace between us now, Korax. But the less often we meet in the future, the happier I will be."

Korax woke to an insistent knocking on his door. "Master, I am so sorry to wake you," Phoemio cried in agitation as he paced into the chamber. "It is Leukon, he has disappeared."

Korax turned in his bed, scowling. A glance through the shutters showed a bright, gray morning. "How long has he been gone?"

"He must have left during the night. Kleis discovered him missing before sunrise. She's frantic with worry."

Next moment, Kleis herself rushed into the room, her hair in disarray, her eyes red from weeping. "I'm sorry to trouble you master. But all his things are gone from his room. I fear he has run away. He's been so gloomy lately, and he would not tell me why. I fear he will do himself evil."

She tore at her hair and wailed pitiably. Korax scratched his head. He hadn't paid much attention to Leukon lately. His life had been peaceful since the trial, quiet winter days passed in relaxation and study. Suddenly, a thought occurred, and he counted the days—just over a month since the winter solstice.

Leukon had served him for a year and a day.

"What shall we do, master?" Phoemio asked helplessly, as Kleis' sobbing rose to a higher pitch.

"Kleis, go back to your work," Korax said. "Phoemio and I will find him. He cannot have gone far."

Phoemio ushered the weeping girl out of the room, and Korax dressed.

A short time later, the two men left the house and hurried down the streets toward the lower city. Korax sent Phoemio to search in the marketplace, while he hunted on the waterfront. Even in an international port like Rhodos, the towering Celt could not wander around unnoticed. Inquiring at the wineshops and brothels west of the Emporium, Korax soon picked up the trail. Before midday, he found Leukon sitting on the edge of a dock, his long legs dangling over the murky water. Beside him lay three wineskins, two of them shriveled and empty.

"You can turn right around and fly back to your uncle's mansion, Blackbird," the Celt declared with drunken bravado. "A year and a day have passed. Leukon is no longer your slave."

"I believe you have reckoned the calendar correctly." Korax sat down a yard away. "Still, you should not have left without telling anyone. Poor Kleis is hysterical."

"I feel sorry for Kleis," Leukon uttered morosely. "She has the misfortune to love a cursed man."

Korax frowned. "You refer to yourself, I suppose. I did not realize you were cursed."

"Sorry! I can say nothing about it." Leukon waved emphatically, then punctuated the gesture with a long swig from his third wineskin.

Korax rolled his eyes at the cloudy heavens. "Suit yourself. By the way, where did you get the money to purchase all this wine?"

"You Greeks are always worried about money! I borrowed a few obols from the strongbox. I will have to pay your uncle back."

"No worry. Consider it a going-away present. So, where are you headed, now that you are free?"

Leukon grunted. "I have no immediate plans. Eventually, I suppose I'll cross to the mainland and hire on with some general."

"I see. Well, you won't be leaving Rhodes till the sailing season, unless you plan on swimming."

Leukon's face declined into a countenance of abject woe. "It makes no difference. The curse follows wherever I go."

"Oh, that again. A pity you can't tell me about this curse. I might be able to help."

"No one can help! Oh, I know you're a wizard, and fairly canny from what I've seen. But this curse is tattooed on the bones of my soul."

"Really? That sounds indelible."

They sat quietly while the seawater slapped the cracked stone of the quay.

"I suppose I should tell you about the curse," Leukon grumbled at last. "You have been a good master, almost a friend. Maybe I owe it to you, before we part."

"I am all ears," Korax said.

Leukon took another long drink. He offered the wine to Korax, who merely shook his head.

"Among my people," Leukon began portentously, "it is a custom sometimes for children to be raised by foster parents. From age three, I was fostered in the house of a chieftain named Kichorios and his wife Rosmerta. They had a son of their own named Aeddon, the same age as me. From boyhood, we were like twins, Aeddon and I. We loved each other like actual brothers— better even. We learned everything together, to hunt and fish and ride, the ancient laws and stories, the sword and the spear. The time came when we were men, and it was proper we should go to war. We lived in the mountains west of Macedonia, in that country you call Illyria. At that time, a chieftain named Bolgios was raising an army. Naturally, Aeddon and I joined him. The night before we left Rosmerta, who loved us both as her sons, laid a geis upon us ..."

"A *geis*, what is that?" Korax asked.

"I know no Greek for it. It is a thing of words, but not a spell or curse. It is a requirement, an obligation. Rosmerta was a powerful woman. She bound Aeddon and me with this geis: that if either of us fell in battle, the survivor must bring his brother's corpse home to her, so she might mourn properly and shed her grief."

"And you swore this as an oath?"

"We had no choice in the matter—It was a geis!"

After guzzling more wine, Leukon continued. His narrative meandered and sometimes sank into maudlin reverie. But eventually, Korax extracted the entire tale.

Leukon and his foster brother followed the chieftain Bolgios into Macedonia, where they raided for two years. Then Bolgios was joined by the armies of two more Celtic lords from the north. The combined force invaded Greece. After penetrating the pass at Thermopylae, the Celts immediately marched on Delphi where, as they well knew, many Greek city-states kept sacred treasuries. The marauders sacked the temple complex and carried off a huge amount of gold and silver: "The treasure of your god Apollo," Leukon called it.

But on their way north the Celts were ambushed. As they crossed a swollen river near the Macedonian border, an alliance of Greek armies attacked them from both banks. Caught by surprise and slowed by the heavy treasure wagons, the Celts were slaughtered. Aeddon took an arrow through the throat. Before Leukon could reach him, his body was swept away by the flood. Leukon struggled out of his armor and dove into the rushing current. He was carried downstream, away from the battle. He searched for three days but never found Aeddon's body.

Disconsolate, he made his way back to the remnants of the Celtic horde as they trudged north, a beaten army. Eventually, he hired on as a mercenary with the new Macedonian king, Antigonus Gonatas. But as soon as he was able, Leukon went back to Illyria to deliver the news of Aeddon's death.

On learning that Leukon had returned without Aeddon's body, his foster mother flew into a frenzy of grief. That night at the chieftain's feast, Rosmerta cursed Leukon: he would be an exile, forced to wander among foreign men, until he brought back the body of his brother.

Leukon departed Illyria the next morning. For the following six years he hired on with one mercenary captain after another, always volunteering for the most dangerous duty, seeking an honorable death in battle, his only possible escape from the curse.

"When our rebellion in Egypt failed and we were trapped on that island, most of my comrades slew themselves with the sword. But the curse would not permit me so easy a death. I thought to drown swimming the Nile, but again the curse did not allow it. Most of the men who reached the shore were speared by cavalry patrols, but I was not so lucky. Because of Rosmerta's curse I ended up in that stinking slave-yard where you found me.

"So now you know my miserable history." Leukon lifted the wineskin for another long gulp.

Korax probed with his mind. Intuition told him that the curse was mostly a matter of belief. If he could change Leukon's thinking about it, he could free the man.

"Remember when we met," he said, "and you learned my name. You decided it was fate, because the crow is sacred to your tribe. Perhaps fortune smiled on you that day, and I am fated to lift your curse. I certainly believe my magic is a match for some old woman of your tribe."

"Don't disrespect Rosmerta," Leukon warned. "The women of my nation are mighty."

"I meant no disrespect. Still, I am certain I can lift the curse—that is, if you want it lifted."

Leukon eyed him with a faint, dubious hope. But then he frowned stubbornly. "No. I know you have power, Blackbird. But this curse is set too deep. It is tattooed—"

"Yes, I know, 'On the bones of your soul.' Well, consider this: It will be two months before any ships leave Rhodos. What will you do in the meantime? Come back to Zeno's house—as a free man—and help Kleis with the garden. You can earn your keep plus enough coin to pay your passage. Meanwhile, let me work on the curse. In two moons, if I have failed to dispel it, you are no worse off, and you are free to go where you will. Is that not a fair bargain?"

The Celt stared sullenly at the lapping water. Finally, he picked up the wineskin. "Let me finish this first. I need to fortify myself if I am going to face Kleis and her tears."

Chapter Eighteen

When Korax returned home with Phoemio and Leukon, the slave Gylon met them at the gate. Zeno had purchased Gylon as his new steward, replacing the renegade Menas. Everyone thought the change a definite improvement, since Gylon was a polite, even-tempered fellow.

"Oh, master Korax. So happy you are back. And you found Leukon; I know Kleis will be relieved. But you have a visitor this afternoon. Halitherses of the House of Philophron has called on you. He is on the upstairs terrace with your father and uncle."

Leaving Phoemio and Gylon to escort Leukon to bed, Korax hurried across the courtyard and up the stairs. He found his father and uncle sitting stiffly in the presence of their aristocratic guest. They lifted their faces with relief at Korax's arrival.

Halitherses stood and inclined his head. "I am happy you have returned, sir. Your father and uncle and I were just discussing our youthful service. All three of us fought against Demetrius at his siege of Rhodos."

Korax made a formal bow. "Pardon my absence, my lord."

"Not at all. Pray forgive my unannounced visit. I understand you were engaged in smoothing out some servant problem. Nothing too bothersome, I trust."

"It is all smoothed out now." Korax took a seat beside his father. "Please, continue your conversation."

As Zeno and Leontes appeared hesitant, Halitherses took the lead. "Well, now that you are here we can, as it were, broach the subject. As I have no wish to waste your time, I will speak bluntly. I have a daughter, Thalia, of marriageable age. As you are no doubt aware, because of past indiscretions, she has incurred certain social liabilities. However, she is a good girl at heart, and I am confident she has learned from her failings and is now ready to be an honorable and dutiful wife. I come today to inquire if you might have any interest in marrying my daughter."

Halitherses lifted a hand. "Before you answer, I must caution that this is not an offer of contract, only an inquiry. I suggested the match to Thalia, and she is not opposed. However, her past mistakes have made her cautious. She would insist on a period of courtship, so you two might know each other better."

"Young people today," Zeno chuckled. "They have their own ideas, that's for certain."

"Indeed, my friend," Halitherses replied. "I sometimes find their modern notions incomprehensible. If your family considers this an imposition, I would certainly understand—"

"On the contrary," Korax interjected. "I think your daughter's position is very sensible. We've only spoken together once, for a few moments."

Halitherses arched his eyebrows, as if that fact seemed completely irrelevant. "Well then, if you are open to the match, I recommend that you visit our home. Feel free to come whenever you wish, and Thalia will receive you. As to the dowry, like many families in Rhodes, ours has struggled these past several years. Still, I would be prepared to settle twenty thousand on Thalia's future husband."

He surveyed their reactions. Leontes and Zeno both made loose-jawed nods of satisfaction. But Korax had other concerns.

"I think the dowry is most generous," he said. "To be frank, I have not given much thought to marriage, as I am still some years under thirty. But one of my concerns regards your son, Patrollos."

"Indeed?" The lord's visage darkened. "You led me to believe the trouble between you was settled."

"It is. Be assured, I harbor no ill will on my side. But Patrollos has made it clear he is uncomfortable in my presence. I don't think he would take it kindly if I married his sister."

"Leave that to me," Halitherses said. "It will not be an issue, I promise. I will not allow Patrollos' pouting to spoil my daughter's happiness."

Korax pondered, scanning the expectant faces of the three elder men. The notion of this marriage was like a thunderbolt from a blue sky.

"My lord, I am sensitive to the great honor you do me and my family. However, I am no less cautious than your daughter. I ask a chance to think it over."

"Of course, that is most sensible of you." Halitherses stood with unhurried dignity. "Feel free to visit my family at any time. All of you gentlemen are always welcome in our house."

He bade them good afternoon. Zeno went to accompany him to the gate. Leontes blinked, looking in Korax's direction.

"What a wonderful development," he exclaimed. "My son, married into the House of Philophron."

Korax sighed. "I meant what I said, father. I really do need to think it over."

"Of course, of course. It is your decision. Still, you could not hope for a more advantageous match. The House of Philophron ..."

The month of Gamelion marked the festival of the sacred marriage of Hera and Zeus. When Korax called on Thalia, he was told he could find her at the guild hall attached to the Temple of Hera. She was working with other women of the town on preparations for the festival.

Korax asked for her at the door of the guild hall. Through the doorway, he observed long tables occupied by girls and women of all ages. Some sewed bright-colored fabric into veils and costumes or tied wreathes of laurel and myrtle. Others rolled and sculpted dough into crescent cakes or carried pans to the kitchen for baking. Presently Thalia came to the door, wearing a greasy apron and a kerchief in her hair.

"Oh, it is you!" She wiped sweat from her brow. "I was told someone had come from my father's house. But I did not expect you."

"I'm sorry to appear unannounced. When I called at your home, your father insisted I visit you here."

"Yes, he's very anxious we become acquainted. I'm sure he was so happy you had called he did not even think about how dreadful I would look."

Korax stepped back. "Perhaps I should visit another time."

"No, it's all right." She removed her apron and hung it on a peg. "Perhaps it's just as well you see me at my worst. It will forestall unpleasant surprises later."

Korax smiled. "You are quite beautiful, Thalia—even at your worst. You need never worry on that account."

"You are very gallant." She pulled off the kerchief and raked a hand through her tangled hair. "We can go and talk in the temple if you like—under the aegis of Hera. That seems appropriate, does it not?"

"Certainly."

They strolled along a covered arcade that led to the steps of the temple. Thalia glanced at her stained gown and laughed.

"How pathetic I am. A girl works so hard to appear attractive to a suitor, and the first time you visit me I look like a kitchen maid."

She reminded Korax a little of Patrollos, full of pride and dignity, yet lacking some essence of self-confidence—as if they constantly measured themselves against some abstract ideal and always came up short.

"The dowry my father offers," she said. "Your family finds it acceptable?"

"Yes, it is quite generous."

She nodded. "My father is very generous with me. But he has also made it clear this is the last time he can give me money. He must consider the inheritance of my two brothers, as well as his old age and that of my mother."

"Then we must make sure this marriage is right for both of us."

"Yes. That is why I insisted on a courtship period. I would rather die unwed than repeat the mistake I made. You are fully aware of my history?"

"I know you were married before, and that your husband made accusations ..."

She paused, halfway up the temple steps. "I will tell you the whole truth. First, I refused to marry the man my father selected for me. That man was old and I found him odious. I was in love with someone else, a charioteer. I married him, against all my family's wishes. But I soon learned he never really loved me, only my father's money. He spent it quickly too, on banquets and courtesans and gambling. The only use he made of me was in his bed, and to show me off to his friends like a prize. One of his companions, another driver, befriended me. His kindness made me feel less lonely, and I let him visit me in my garden. I swear, I never slept with him. Though honestly, I cannot swear it wouldn't have happened eventually. But my husband caught us together. That night, he got drunk and beat me with his fists. I had never been hurt like that, and I swore I never would be again. As soon as he fell asleep, I left his house. I have not allowed him near me since."

"You were right to leave," Korax affirmed. "I have been a slave, and I know what it is to be beaten without redress. I never inflict that on my slaves, and would certainly not inflict it on my wife, under any circumstances."

"I believe you." Her voice trembled a little. She started up the steps. "Now you know my story, but I still know mostly rumors about you. And there are many wild rumors."

"Ask me what you will," Korax replied with a muted laugh. "I will try to be as honest as you."

"Are you a sorcerer?"

"No. That word implies a practitioner of harmful rites."

"A mage then?"

"A student of the Mysteries."

They crossed the portico and passed through the open doorway, into the cool interior. At the front of the chamber, the image of Hera looked down from a gold and ivory throne. Korax and Thalia stopped at the back row of pillars. They bowed their heads respectfully to the queen of the gods.

"So you do revere the gods?" Thalia whispered.

"Yes, of course."

She eyed him sidewise in the dim hall. "It frightens me a little that you study strange philosophies. You are not like anyone else I know."

"I understand. But if we decide to marry, I promise to care for you and treat you as any honorable gentleman of Rhodes treats his wife. My studies should not affect our marriage in any way."

She gave him a penetrating, doubtful look. "I will have to think about that. But for my part, if we decide to marry, I will do my best to be a dutiful wife, to care for your house and your children—if Hera blesses us with children. I will try not to overspend or make unreasonable demands on you."

She glanced up at the statue of the goddess, then lowered her eyes. "I know there is a hetaera that you visit. I would not expect you to give her up. Still, a woman has her pride. I will tell you frankly, our marriage will not be happy if you spend many nights with other women."

"The hetaera you mention is a dear friend and will always be," Korax said. "But I am no profligate, and I would never dishonor you with licentious or indiscreet behavior."

Thalia's full lips pressed together. "I would not wish to become a bitter, jealous wife. Still, I insist on being treated with respect. You must understand that I have a will and a mind of my own."

Korax grinned. "I have no objection to that. There is a history of strong-willed women in my family."

Her face brightened. "Good. Perhaps you will find me appealing then."

"Oh, I do already." He reached for her hand. "Are your feelings in accord? Should I call again to continue the courtship?"

She looked around to be sure they were alone. Then she stood on her toes, threw her arms around his neck and kissed him sweetly on the mouth.

"Please do call again," she whispered. She gave him a playful expression, then turned and departed with a quick, light-footed gait.

Korax insisted Leukon fast for three days before the next full moon. He kept the Celt locked in a downstairs storeroom and gave him only water. He instructed Leukon to think about nothing except what his life would be like without the curse.

At twilight on the night of the full moon, Leukon bathed in cool water scented with magical herbs. Korax anointed the strong, fair-skinned body with a mixture of pungent oils. The fumes made him lightheaded, which was exactly the effect he hoped to induce in the Celt. Leukon stood stoically while Korax blindfolded him and tied his wrists with a black silk cord.

Korax led him out to the courtyard, just as the moon was rising. He set him to stand immobile and silent in the center of the garden path. He burned chunks of fragrant cedar wood in three iron braziers. Amid the thick smoke, he circled Leukon, uttering a chant, occasionally touching the Celt's nude body with the tip of his olive-wood wand.

He visualized the curse as an entity, a serpent of yellow light coiled around Leukon's spine. Slowly, he loosened the coils with his will.

He continued the rite until the moon set and the faint light of dawn was growing. Then, gathering his power, Korax spoke magic words and touched the wand to the Celt's chest. In his mind he saw the curse flutter and blink out like a candle.

Exhausted, he took a knife and cut away the cords and blindfold. "The curse is lifted," he declared, weary but triumphant.

Leukon scowled and peered inwardly.

"No, it isn't," he said at last. "But I see now how it might be, in time."

Korax stared at him, baffled. "What do you see?"

"If my ancestors decide to forgive me, I may be given another chance. Then, if I succeed, the curse will be lifted."

Korax lowered himself onto a bench.

"Do not feel dejected," Leukon told him. "You have done the best you could."

The salon had ended and only a few guests lingered in the banquet hall and on the terrace. Korax leaned his elbows on the balustrade, gazing into Berenicea's darkened garden. Inside, someone plucked on a lyre. The night air was fragrant with the first blooms of spring.

"There's my love." Berenicea kissed him on the cheek. "You seemed distracted all evening, and now you look moody."

"Pondering a decision," Korax said.

"Does it concern your marriage?"

Korax straightened. "So you've heard?"

"Oh, my dear, I hear all the gossip. And there is plenty concerning you and Thalia."

"Really?"

"Of course: the notorious daughter of Philophron and the conjurer who saved Rhodes from the clutches of Amynias—a most juicy romance."

He smiled, but felt a pang of melancholy. "She is a sweet girl, really. I am almost ready to commit to the contract."

"What makes you hesitate?"

"I'm not sure ... Settling down with a wife, helping to run the family business, when I was a slave, if I had thought my life would lead to such a place, it would have seemed impossibly wonderful. Now, somehow, I'm dissatisfied and restless."

"Do you miss Alexandria?"

"In a way. Not that I would go back, even if I could."

"Perhaps you have not recovered from your experiences there and are not yet ready to love a wife."

"Perhaps." He gazed into her compassionate face. "But when I examine all that's occurred since I returned to Rhodes, I realize my happiest moments have been spent with you."

Berenicea embraced him and kissed his lips. "My dear, I will always be your friend."

"But never my wife."

She hugged him tighter, and her voice had a mournful edge. "O my dear Odysseus, if we live many lives, as some sages claim, then perhaps the gods will grant us that favor, in some other time and place."

Chapter Nineteen

Zeus sent abundant rains in the early spring, raising verdant growth in the gardens and parks of Rhodos and on the hills above the town. The wedding of Korax and Thalia was set for the festival at midsummer. But Korax had little time to think about his impending marriage.

His days were hurried and cluttered with business activities. The wealth that came to him in the settlement of Amynias' property was much more than he expected. It included both his father's old house and the farmstead up in the highlands. Korax thought to keep the townhouse and eventually live there with Thalia. But first he intended a complete refurbishing, and a magical cleansing of Amynias' evil emanations. On the other hand, he saw no use at all for a farm and planned to sell or rent that property.

But he made little progress dealing with those matters. As the sailing season loomed, he negotiated with bankers and merchants, studied contracts, plotted shipping schedules. While Zeno and Leontes both participated in the meetings, they left more and more of the work in Korax's hands.

The moon of Dionysus drew near, and Korax looked forward to the festival. At least for a few days, he would be able to forget his work, attend plays and celebrations, visit with Thalia and her family.

But a fortnight before the Dionysia, a plume of smoke arose beyond the acropolis, far to the south. People gathered in the marketplace and observed it from their housetops, speculating in hushed concern on what it might mean. Staring at the smoke from the roof of Zeno's house, Korax felt a premonition of disaster.

Next morning, word arrived that pirates had sacked Kamiros. Fishing boats from the town had made their way up the coast with a handful of survivors. A bit later, dozens of refugees straggled into Rhodos from the overland road. The news spread quickly through the city.

That afternoon, the Assembly and the Council met in a combined session. Korax, Zeno, and Isochomachus walked down the hill and joined the fretful, murmuring crowd that filled the square outside the Assembly Hall. They conversed with neighbors and fellow citizens, listened to the worried talk, tried to sort truth from rumor. This much seemed clear: Pirates had surprised Kamiros at dawn, arriving at a time of year when most seamen still avoided crossing open water due to fogs and the threat of storms. If a Rhodian squadron patrolled nearby, it was quickly overwhelmed by the pirate fleet. Scores of men had been killed, hundreds of women and children carried off. It was said parts of the town were burned to the ground, all except the acropolis plundered.

A chill rain started to fall, but the crowd lingered in the square and adjacent porticoes. From time to time, an official emerged and was immediately surrounded by a mob demanding information. A dazed feeling of unreality hovered everywhere. To Korax it was palpable, like a choking vapor. It was the first time in memory a Rhodian town had been sacked. Kamiros stood only a day's sail from Rhodos. If the brigands could strike there, no place was safe.

But what could be done? That was the question everyone wanted answered. There was talk of sending an expedition to Crete to hunt down the pirates, perhaps rescue the captives. But that had been tried before without success. Confronted by Rhodian squadrons, the pirates typically fled in their swift hemiolias, then waited in ambush among the coves and headlands of their coast. They knew the winds and currents around Crete far better than the

Rhodians. Besides, to send a significant force would mean leaving the coast of Rhodes unguarded.

At dusk, an archon and an admiral came out on the steps to address the people. But their vague, reassuring speeches did little to calm the disquiet. Only nightfall finally dispersed the crowd.

Korax trudged soberly up the hill with his uncle and cousin. Arriving home, they were met at the gate by the entire household, everyone shouting questions at once.

"What did you learn?" Leontes demanded.

"Is it true the whole city was destroyed?" Callipatria cried.

"It is monstrous beyond belief," Phoemio said, "truly frightening. How will Rhodes survive?"

"Will there be war?" Leukon asked. "Will we fight?"

"We don't have any answers," Zeno told them wearily. "But something will be done, I promise you. Rhodes will not let this atrocity go unpunished. Don't you agree, Korax?"

"Yes. Something must be done."

They took a quiet, grim supper of barley bread and dried fish. Korax avoided drinking any wine. As soon as possible, he retired to his chamber and lit candles on his altar. He burned incense before the electrum statue of Athene and sat down to quiet his mind.

But the peace of meditation did not come. Visions of the fall of Kamiros blazed in his brain: the flames of burning houses, screams of women, groans of dying men. Then memories flooded in: he saw himself after he was seized by the pirates, chained in the dank belly of a hemiolia. Later, other captives were herded in, wailing in despair.

Korax opened his eyes, his breath heaving. He tried to summon Athene, but instead another voice sounded in his mind—far away, yet strong and brazen as a trumpet.

"My son, the time has come. You are called to the service of Rhodes."

Helios. Korax sensed the god's power throbbing in his blood. Dread arose, as if a profound, inescapable destiny was suddenly at hand.

"But how? How can I serve?"

The god's answer came in the form of thoughts. Sailing with the fleet, Korax could use his scrying skills to discern the position of pirate vessels, help the commanders hunt them down. Then another, stranger thought occurred …

Korax took a lamp and searched through his basket of scrolls. Many of these magical books he had not examined since leaving Alexandria. He untied ribbons and opened rolls till finding the one he sought. It was a compendium of ancient texts translated from the Babylonian. Near the end of the roll he found these formulas:

The Means of Calling Wind and Rain
The Means of Dispelling a Tempest
The Means of Raising Fog for Concealment

He remembered copying the texts in the Paneum library, during that period when he explored all possible avenues of magic. Of course, the idea of mastering the weather was an old and venerable one. Korax had always viewed it with skepticism: so much of magical lore was rife with hyperbole and outright fraud. Now, as he read the texts, the notion seemed incredible.

"No," Helios told him. "My power lives in you. But *your will* must direct it into the mortal world."

If this were possible … What greater weapon in a naval campaign than the power to conjure wind and storm?

Deliberately, Korax slowed his breathing. Presently he set down the papyrus, stood and stripped off his chiton. He traced a circle on the floor with a piece of charcoal. After placing a candle and censer in the center, he used a dagger to trace another circle, an envisioned ring of gleaming blue. On the edges of this ring he drew sigils of elemental Air, then sat down and chanted quietly. He conjured a daimon he had spoken with in the past, a spirit of the upper air. Soon, the winged creature fluttered before his mind's eye, with pale blue skin and blowing yellow hair.

"Nomarabek, Lion of the Air," Korax whispered. "I know your true name."

"Tell me your will, O wise and potent mage."

"Fair and lovely spirit, tell me this: Is it possible for a mortal to command the wind and rain."

"Depending on the god or spirit who lends you power."

"Is it possible for me, with the might of Helios that I have?"

The daimon squinted with concentration. "On land but not on sea."

"Why not on the sea?"

"The Lord of the Sun is with you, but the Lord of the Sea opposes you." Suddenly, Nomarabek's eyes opened wide with consternation. "He comes! Farewell."

The winged daimon vanished, and a thundering sea wave swept over the envisioned space. It crashed over Korax, and he felt the cold splash on his skin, the stinging brine in his nostrils. As he fought to regain his breath, an immense green figure loomed before him, a terrible visage with drenched, tangled hair, dripping beard, and round, yellow eyes. Korax flinched before the naked immensity of the god. His spirit was miniscule in comparison, a minnow in the sea. How could a mortal ever hope to challenge such power?

The baleful eyes of Poseidon fixed on him. Then a force like a team of horses flung him to his back, and the dagger flew from his hand. His body stiffened and shuddered. It seemed he was drowning, sinking into a dark abyss. The light of the surface dwindled far overhead, and his soul knew the torment of utter despair.

He woke, weak and dizzy, a fearful aching in his joints. He lurched to the balcony and pulled open the doors. The first glimmer of dawn hung faint and silver in the east.

Revived by the air, he crept back into his room. He lit a fresh candle on Athene's altar and sat down before her image. His fingers groped along his neck and temples, rubbing gently as he tried to dispel the throbbing pain.

When he managed to quiet his thoughts, Athene came to him.

"As you have seen, Poseidon's enmity is roused. He considers your intention a usurping of divine power."

"Yet Helios calls me to this course—Helios and my own sense of duty. What am I to do, goddess?"

"That must be your decision."

"But ... Can I succeed?"

"That is hard to say. When gods contest in strife, mortals are often caught in the chaos. Sometimes they shift the flow; other times they are trampled and destroyed. I must warn you, Korax, if you venture onto the sea, I can give you little aid. That is Poseidon's realm, and there he is supreme."

Korax opened his eyes and stared at the figure of the goddess. "Success seems unlikely in any case. I'd have to convince the navy to let me sail, to work magic on one of their warships. It sounds ridiculous. Likely as not, they will scorn the idea."

"They are in dire need of help," Athene pointed out. "If you suggest only that you can assist in finding their quarry, they may give you a readier welcome."

"Yes, you are right." Korax pondered. The dread destiny he had sensed earlier was directly in front of him now.

Athene said: "I once told you that you might surprise yourself one day and prove a hero. The time has come to answer that question."

Korax let his eyes fall shut. No further talk was needed. "Wise goddess, I thank you for your counsel, as always."

When dawn came, Korax dressed in a fresh chiton of Athenian wool and a gray chlamys. He fastened on a pair of sandals and slung his sword-belt over his shoulder. Before leaving his room, he put on his protective amulet.

In the pale morning, he marched down the hill of Rhodos to the manor house of Philophron. But it was not Thalia that he asked for when the sleepy gatekeeper let him into the courtyard. Soon Patrollos descended the steps, his chiton unbelted, his curly hair uncombed. He stared at Korax in confusion.

"I must speak with you," Korax said. "It is vital."

Chapter Twenty

On a hill above the barracks and workshops of the military harbor stood a fortified citadel. Patrollos led Korax up a succession of steep lanes and steps. Wearied by headache and lack of sleep, Korax had difficulty matching Patrollos' brisk, determined gait.

They gained the summit and strode along a high colonnade. Observing Patrollos in his officer's armor, the sentries straightened and stamped their pikes in salute. At the middle of the porch, Patrollos stopped before stout doors ribbed with iron.

"Wait here," he told Korax. "I will let you know."

Korax wandered to the edge of the portico and gazed down at the harbor. Scores of warships rode at anchor, the pride of the Rhodian navy. Men moved on the planks and decks of a number of the ships, loading provisions, stowing gear.

Suddenly Korax lurched and propped his arm on a pillar. His head was swimming, his legs weak. He blinked and squinted. Whatever violence the sea god had inflicted on his body, he was not yet fully recovered.

"Are you all right?" Patrollos hovered beside him with a stern expression.

"Yes."

"Come then. The admiral has agreed to see you."

Korax followed him into a high-roofed chamber, lit by tall, columned windows set along the top of mural-covered walls. Long tables stood cluttered with maps and documents, pored over by clusters of navy officers. Couriers hurried back and forth, and scribes recorded orders on tablets.

At the far end of the chamber, Patrollos presented Korax to Admiral Nicocles. A stout, affable man with a neatly-clipped beard, Nicocles was dressed informally in a gray chiton and leathern belt. Korax knew him by reputation, one of four admirals in the Rhodian navy, and among the few men from outside the nobility to ever attain that rank.

"I recognize you sir, I attended your trial," the admiral said. "Unfortunately, ridding ourselves of your cousin's treachery did not cripple the pirates as much as we hoped. Some even speculate they sacked Kamiros in reprisal for the confiscation of their bank accounts."

A new wave of dizziness assailed Korax. He leaned both hands on the table. "I realize you are busy, my lord, so I will not waste your time. I believe you are planning to sail against the brigands."

Nicocles glanced sharply at Patrollos. "That has been discussed but no announcement made."

"Is my understanding incorrect?" Korax pressed.

"I told him nothing," Patrollos asserted. "Nothing he did not already know. Korax has ... an art for learning things. I believe that is his point in coming to us."

Nicocles turned back to Korax, brows arched expectantly.

"Patrollos speaks the truth," Korax said. "I have certain skills. And I was a prisoner once in Crete. Between my knowledge of their coasts, and my ability as a seer, I believe I can help you find the pirate squadrons. I request the honor of sailing with you."

The admiral showed him a dubious, appraising frown. After a moment, he tilted his head. "Come with me."

They stepped to a nearby table where a detailed map of Crete lay unrolled.

"You were held prisoner by the brigands? Show me where."

Korax traced his finger over the map, pointing to a cove. "I believe it was here. This stretch of coast looks familiar. But finding their strongholds will be less difficult than catching and destroying their ships."

"Indeed. What can you tell me of the currents and winds?"

"I arrived in the month Elaphebolion, and the southerlies were already blowing. This early, I'd expect erratic winds. The current flowed mainly this way."

"You are a seaman, I'll allow that much," Nicocles said. "And you are correct about the winds. They shift often this time of year, prevailing breezes from the south, squalls from any quarter."

Looking up from the map, he confronted Korax bluntly. "This voyage will be dangerous, sir. We're commissioning four squadrons to sail the day after tomorrow: twenty galleys plus two supply ships. Our plan is to sweep the seas north of Crete and return south of the island. We'll destroy any pirate craft we find, at sea or on the beaches. But with only twenty warships, if the Cretans make a stand, we'll likely be outnumbered—perhaps by two or three to one. Then I'll have to decide whether to risk battle, or if we're the ones who must run. It is a desperate plan. The Council is sending only as many ships as they feel they can afford to lose and still defend our coasts. The men sailing on this voyage stand a good chance of not coming back."

"I understand the risk," Korax said.

"You look pale, sir. Are you sick?"

Korax swallowed, his throat raw. "I had a sleepless night. But I am fit to sail."

"I see. I must admit, chasing down the pirates, knowing where they may be lying in wait for us—those are difficult problems. Do you really think your skills might help us?"

"I do, my lord, or I would not be here."

The admiral pondered, still unsure. He cast his eyes on Patrollos. "He's your friend, Commander. What is your view?"

Patrollos looked startled by the question, or perhaps by the declaration that Korax was his friend. "I ... know nothing of the arts he practices. But I can vouch for his bravery and honor, without hesitation."

"I see." Nicocles turned back to Korax. "You've had your naval training?"

"Only my first year at the oars. But I've kept up my arms training. Also, I have a companion who is skilled at arms. He has soldiered for both Macedonia and Egypt. I expect he will want to sail with me."

Nicocles peered into Korax's eyes a moment longer, then nodded. "Since you understand the risks, even if there is only the slightest chance your abilities can aid us, I see no reason to refuse your offer. You and your man will sail as deck-fighters on my flagship."

Phoemio grunted as he tightened the cords of the cuirass. "It's a little loose, master. Couldn't you as least find one that fit you?"

The cuirass was gray, two plates of stiffened linen laced together at the shoulders, armpits and waist. Korax had never worn armor before.

"It's the nearest the armory had to my size. Poor Leukon will have to go without one."

"Oh, I don't worry about Leukon," Phoemio said. "It will take more than Cretan arrows to pierce his thick hide."

There had been no time to have armor custom-made of course, so Korax had purchased equipment for himself and Leukon from the storerooms of the naval armory. The past two days had flown by in a blur of frantic activity—packing his scrolls and magical tools, making sacrifice at the temples, commissioning Staphylus to draw up his will.

Phoemio pinned the naval cloak at his shoulder. Korax set the bronze helmet over his head and fixed the strap at his chin. At least the helmet was a good fit. Phoemio stepped back to examine him. Suddenly, tears filled the slave's eyes.

"Well, I suppose you had better go now. But be sure to say good-bye to your father, please. He will blame me if you don't."

"I will," Korax said.

Leukon stepped out to the courtyard in the chilly morning. Kleis had gone to work early. She knelt in a plot of soil, tying new grape vines up on stakes. Leukon leaned his pike and javelins against the wall and set his buckler and helmet on a bench. He walked quietly over to her.

"Korax has come down. We'll be leaving in a moment."

She refused to turn around.

"Aren't you going to tell me good-bye?"

"Good-bye."

The Celt rolled his eyes unhappily. "Kleis, must you be so stubborn? I told you why I must go. Even though I'm no longer a bondsman, until I hire on with someone else Korax counts as my chieftain. I cannot let him go to war alone, on my honor."

"You don't owe me an explanation. I'm just a slave girl you've slept with. I have no pledge from you."

He crouched beside her. "There is another reason. I prayed to my ancestors for an opportunity, and now this war has come. It might be my chance to lift the curse."

"Good. I wish you well."

"You don't understand. If I can lift the curse, I can come back to you a free man."

She paused, the stake trembling in her hand. Then she stabbed it into the damp earth. "You'd better go."

Leukon sighed, shaking his head. He rose and stepped away, then halted. Abruptly, he picked her up and hugged her fiercely.

"No!" Kleis tried to push him away. But his strong arms trapped her and soon her struggles ceased. Her arms encircled his back. She leaned her head on his chest and wept.

Korax met his aunt and uncle in the foyer below the grand stair.

"Are you sure you don't want us to come down to the harbor to see you off," Zeno said. "Your father's not up to making the trip, but Callipatria and I could come."

"It's just as well to say our good-byes here. Is my father not up yet?"

Zeno and Callipatria glanced woefully at each other.

"He claims he can't bear to see you," Callipatria explained. "He is finding it hard to accept that you are going, Korax. He does not understand why you must."

"I know. I will try again to explain it to him."

Moving stiffly in the unfamiliar armor, Korax hurried back up the steps. He knocked on his father's door then pushed it open. Leontes lay on his bed in the gloom, staring at the light between the shutter slats.

Korax sat on the bed and clutched the old man's bony hand. "Father, I've come to say farewell. I hope you will give me your blessing."

Leontes' face contorted. "I-I can't. I know you feel you must do this, Korax, but I cannot agree. Joining the militia to guard the city walls as Isochomachus is doing—that I could understand. But not sailing to Crete with attack squadrons. You are not a military man. It is senseless."

"I realize it is hard to understand. But I must do this for Rhodes, because no one else can."

"Magic again! Your mother's cursed arts. You practiced magic irresponsibly as a youth, and it brought us all to grief. Now you claim you must use magic out of duty. I say it is madness and will only bring us grief again."

Korax squeezed his father's hand. "When you were a young man, you fought on the walls against Demetrius, because it was your duty. We must all defend Rhodes as best we are able. This is something I am able to do."

Leontes moaned and cast his hands in the air. "I lost my first two sons to the sea. I lost your mother. You returned last year, and I've only just begun to have hope again for the future. Now you are sailing off, probably to your death. The gods have inflicted too much sorrow on me, Korax. It is more than I can bear."

Korax's heart sank. "I must go now, father. Please give me your blessing."

Leontes tightened his lips. "I'm sorry, but I cannot."

"Farewell, then."

Korax rose and marched across the room. He was almost out the door when Leontes called to him.

"Wait, Korax! Wait! I give you my blessing. I cannot let you go without it. If that is what I can do for Rhodes, then I will do it. I give you my blessing."

Korax returned and kissed his father's hands.

By mid-morning the sun burned orange in a white, misty sky. Crowds of well-wishers lined the avenue leading to the military harbor. The citizens of Rhodos had recovered from the first shock of the pirate attack and now their warlike spirit was roused. They cheered and shouted encouragement at the sailors, rowers, and deck-fighters who passed through the harbor gates.

Korax and Leukon walked together, carrying their round shields and pikes. Leukon had a long quiver of javelins slung over his broad shoulder. Behind them, two porters bore a wicker basket filled mostly with Korax's gear.

They passed along the crowded quay, filled with the sounds of flutes, laughter and weeping; the smells of perfume and sweat, pitch and the sea. To Korax the scene felt vividly unreal. Three days ago, his only concerns were balancing accounts and booking cargoes. Now he prepared to board a fighting ship, bound for war and probably his doom.

Dry-mouthed, he approached the admiral's high-decked quinquereme, the *Epicherse*. Sailors and marines stood clustered on the dock, bidding goodbye to family and friends. Korax spotted Patrollos holding the hands of a slender woman in white. It was Berenicea, her hair concealed by the veil of her himation. He thought he would like to bid her farewell and wondered if he might wait till Patrollos finished.

Then someone hailed him.

"Greetings to you, sir. Permit us the honor of commending your valor and wishing you a safe voyage."

Korax bowed to Halitherses, his wife Choronice, and Thalia. "I thank you, my lord, ladies."

Thalia gazed at him intently.

"Perhaps you would like a word alone with my daughter," Halitherses suggested. "I'm sure that would be all right."

He and his wife tactfully withdrew. Korax sent Leukon up the gangplank with the porters.

"When Patrollos told me you were sailing with him," Thalia said, "I was surprised."

Korax bowed his head. "Please forgive me. I should have come and explained. It was grossly unfair of me."

"You must have much on your mind," Thalia said, trying to hide her hurt. "I hope you do not mind my speaking with you."

"Of course not. No one in my family understands why I am going. I hope you can understand."

Her moist eyes traveled up the painted wales and tall mast. "The men in my family have always served in the navy. I have lost dear uncles and cousins. I know all about Karpathos and Kamiros. If you can help them, of course you must go."

Korax reached for her hand. "You are noble and brave, Thalia. I will be proud to have you for my wife."

She smiled faintly. "A woman's duty is to face such times with courage. If I've learned nothing else of honor from my family, I know that much. I have asked Patrollos to watch out for you. I ask you the same: Protect my brother, if you can."

Korax kissed the back of her hand. "I promise, I will do my best to protect us all."

Chapter Twenty-One

When Korax reached the deck, his porters had already departed. Rowers carried their kits to the companionways, while marines stowed weapons on deck and crewmen made ready to sail. Leukon sat on the wicker basket, hand cupping his chin, watching the hurried activity with an imperturbable expression.

The *Epicherse* was a quinquereme, among the largest Rhodian warships, with fighting turrets and raised decks at stem and stern. While Leukon would sleep under awnings with the deck-fighters, Korax had been assigned a cabin, a private place for practicing his arts. Leukon picked up the basket and followed Korax aft.

The boatswain directed them to the cabin, below the rear-deck. It was a tiny compartment set against the hull, across a gangway from the captain's quarters. A narrow bunk on the wall took up half the space. Leukon had to set the basket on the bunk in order for both of them to squeeze inside.

"Not very spacious," the Celt remarked.

Still, he sat down on the floor, making Korax climb around him to unpack. Korax did not mind at all.

"I'm glad you decided to take this voyage," he said. "Somehow I feel safer with you along."

"So you should," Leukon answered, his sheathed long sword resting against his thigh. "I am more than a match for a whole ship full of brigands."

"Of that, I have no doubt."

Korax took a tapestry from the top of the basket. He hooked it over the bunk as a bed curtain.

Curiously, Leukon eyed the fabric, a pattern of interwoven spiral designs. "I've not seen that cloth before. It looks like the weaving of the eastern Celts."

"It comes from my mother's people in Thrace. It used to hang on my wall when I was a boy." Korax had brought it because it reminded him of his mother. He hoped it would help him invoke her protection.

"Yes," Leukon said, "I remember being told that your mother was from Thrace. Some say the Thracian tribes are related to the Celts, you know."

"I've heard that," Korax replied. "Many of them do have red hair and blue eyes."

Leukon grinned with delight. "So maybe we are distant kinsmen then? That fits. That clearly makes sense."

"Fits how?" Korax asked. "What do you mean?"

"Oh, nothing." The Celt moved fluidly to his feet. "I will leave you to unpack." He ducked his head and slipped noiselessly through the doorway.

As the warships embarked, the priests of the city made offerings and prayed to Poseidon, Athene, Helios, and Zeus. The squadrons rowed in formation through the mouth of the harbor, while the crowds on the docks sang hymns. As the flotilla passed out of sight and the people began to disperse, some citizens walked to the water's edge and offered personal prayers and sacrifices.

One of these was Berenicea, the hetaera and priestess of Aphrodite. She poured a libation of golden Cyprian wine into the harbor and called aloud on her goddess.

"Beloved Aphrodite, born of the foaming waves, guide and protect the men of Rhodes on the sea. And guard in particular my two heroes, my two loves: Patrollos, my dear Achilles, and Korax, my Odysseus. Protect them, dear goddess, and bring them home safely to the city they love and to those who love them."

Shutting her eyes, Berenicea breathed in the salt breeze and felt the life of the goddess calm her spirit.

At last, she turned to leave. But along with her servants, someone else watched her, a small young woman with golden hair and eyes red from crying.

"That was beautiful," she murmured. "I am Thalia."

"I know who you are, my lady."

"I knew that Patrollos and Korax both love you. But I did not realize how you also love them."

Berenicea smiled. "You did not think a woman like me capable of such love?"

"No … Please forgive me, I meant no insult." Thalia started to withdraw.

"Wait." Berenicea approached her. "I took no offense."

Thalia peered into the hetaera's eyes. "May I ask you a question, priestess?"

"Of course."

"Mistress Thalia! Your parents sent me to find you." One of the woman servants from the House of Philophron called from a few yards away. "It is time to go home now."

"Tell them I will be there in a moment," Thalia said.

"Mistress, you should not be speaking with … that woman."

"I will come in a moment. Go!"

The servant scowled but turned and bustled off.

"What is your question?" Berenicea asked.

"Why are they both so in love with you? You are very beautiful, of course. But so are many other women. I feel there must be more to it."

"They are my friends, but they are not in love with me, not in the way you mean. Patrollos responds to the goddess, because she loves him so much, loves his weakness as well as his strength. And Korax—Well, he just needs a place to rest his head." She ended with a fond smile.

But Thalia frowned in confusion. "I do not understand you."

Berenicea sighed. "They do not love *me*, but the goddess within me. I am simply her vessel. And men adore *her* because, whatever love they bring, she blesses and makes them feel it is wonderful, and that it is enough."

"But, then ... is there nothing for you?"

"Oh, yes." Berenicea said. "There is service and sacrifice, but also much joy. Because I feel Aphrodite's love inside me every day. And she loves the whole world."

Thalia blinked and shook her head. "I am no priestess, and I could never be so selfless. I fear no one will ever love me the way Korax loves you."

Berenicea stared at her, as if listening to a whisper. "I suggest you pray to the goddess. Ask her to fill your heart. I feel that ... first she must teach you to love yourself. After that, well, you may be surprised." Smiling kindly, she caressed the girl's hair with both hands, then bent and kissed her forehead. "I give you her blessing, dear child."

The priestess straightened, to find Thalia's eyes shining with fresh tears.

Nicocles' fleet comprised twenty-two ships, mainly sleek triremes and quadriremes with multiple banks of oars and deadly bronze-sheathed rams. Two swift penteconters, light galleys with fifty oarsmen each, rode on the flanks as scouts. Two freighters completed the flotilla, a necessity since the warships carried only enough food and water for three days at sea. Powered only by mainsail, the supply ships had to be towed when the fleet relied on oars. Each freighter carried an extra contingent of fighting men, fifty marines and fifty slingers.

Moving under oars, the fleet rounded the northern tip of Rhodes. With a favorable breeze astern, the ships then hoisted sail. They cruised southwest along the coast, formed in two lines with the supply ships in the rear. They passed the town of Ialysos at midday and raised Kamiros in the late afternoon. Nicocles made it a point to sail close to the plundered city.

All hands lined the rails and a morbid quiet settled over the flagship. Korax and Leukon watched from the rear deck as the crumbled, blackened ruins drifted by. Korax glanced at the men near him—Patrollos, Cimon, other officers and helmsmen. In all of their faces he saw the reflection of his own shock and outrage.

"Take a good look," Nicocles shouted, striding along the main deck. "Look hard and remember."

At nightfall the flotilla anchored in the straits between Rhodes and the small island of Alimia. Locked in his cabin, Korax perused his magical texts and attempted the discipline of calling and dispelling winds. The might of Helios lived in him, indeed it burned in his blood like a low, constant fever. But whenever Korax focused his mind at the inner place of power, he sensed a sinister presence, the grim and angry sea-god.

Here, away from the land, Poseidon seemed pervasive and all-powerful. Korax likened himself to a castaway, adrift on writhing waves. His magic might make him a good swimmer, but he had nothing to cling to. Eventually, overcome by exhaustion, he must sink into the deep. He slept fitfully that night, tossing and twisting in the cramped bunk, dreaming of his death.

At dawn the fleet struck off across the open sea, a straight-line course that would take them past Karpathos to the eastern tip of Crete. They sailed in a double-V formation, the penteconters on the wings, the *Epicherse* in the center.

On the main deck, Korax and Leukon drilled and practiced with Patrollos' marines. The fighters seemed much impressed with the Celt's size, agility and deft handling of the pike. Korax they found much less formidable.

Toward midday the wind died, then started blowing from the opposite direction. The captains gave orders to lower sail, and the rowers ran out their oars. Rowing in shifts, the flotilla continued on against the wind and choppy water, their speed reduced from seven or eight knots to two.

Next day, with the rocky coast of Karpathos off to port, lookouts spotted a hemiolia. A trumpet sounded the alarm, and signal flags climbed the rigging of the forward ships. The hemiolia was sailing a reach on an easterly course, patrolling. Spying the Rhodian fleet, she dropped sail and turned south, putting out her oars. Nicocles ordered the green flag run up his mast, the command to pursue.

Below the decks of the Rhodian ships, all the rowers swarmed to their benches. Except for the galleys that towed the supply ships, the whole fleet joined the charge. Oars churned the water, and the galleys spurted to attack speed.

On board the quinquereme, Korax and Leukon armed themselves. They took their stations amidships and watched from the rail as the powerful Rhodian galleys slowly closed the gap on the hemiolia.

Then the Rhodian artillery came into play. Darts and stones arced through the sky, launched from ballistas on the forward quadriremes. The first missiles splashed in the water, but soon the artillerymen found the range. Barbed darts raked the deck of the pirate vessel and stones smashed her benches. As rowers were killed by the onslaught, the hemiolia lost speed. The Cretans answered with a volley of arrows as soon as the first Rhodian craft drew close. But by now the hemiolia could barely maneuver. A trireme raced across the water and rammed her side. When the trireme disengaged, the pirate began to sink.

Most of the Cretans went down with their ship, shooting arrows to the last. A few jumped from the wreck and swam to the nearest galleys. The Rhodian marines showed them no mercy, skewering the pirates with long pikes as they tried to clamber onboard.

But even as the fight ended, two more hemiolias were spied in the distance, already running south. Word passed quickly up the Rhodian line till it reached the flagship.

Nicocles shaded his eyes and scanned the sea. The pirates were specks on the horizon.

"Will we pursue?" Patrollos asked.

The admiral glanced over his shoulder, grimaced as he spotted his freighters far in the rear. "No. We can't risk dispersing the fleet or losing touch with our supply ships."

The green flag came down and the blue was raised, the signal to reset the formation.

Watching from the main deck, Leukon grasped the tactical situation. "Those ships will escape and warn their fellow brigands in Crete."

Korax's voice was heavy with foreboding. "No question. They will know we are coming."

Chapter Twenty-Two

Ribbed slabs of oxen, lamb, and goat cooked slowly over the fire pit. The high-roofed hall was filled with boisterous shouting and laughter. Over a hundred pirate captains and crewmen sprawled at low tables, slurped wine and squeezed the flesh of slave girls. Veiled women danced before a low dais at the front of the hall, to the shrill music of pipes and drums. From the head table, the eight chiefs of the pirate guild watched the dance. All were muscular, battle-scarred men with braided hair and triple-rings in their ears.

A ninth man also shared their table. He was the guild's banker, Amynias—formerly of Rhodos, late of Halicarnassus, now an honored guest in Crete. Owing to an injury of which he would say little, the pirates had taken to calling him *Amynias One-Arm*.

He surveyed the feast hall with a thin-lipped visage. The Cretans were savages of course, their customs barbaric, their personal habits vile. But they were savages who had earned Amynias a lot of money and with whom he expected to make much more. This summer he would sail as their financial agent, to invest their wealth at the great banking cities of Athens, Ephesus, and Pergamon. For now, he must suffer their hospitality and play the part of grateful guest.

The dancers finished, gathered up their veils and scampered away. Ephoros, the lord of the hall, leaned toward Amynias with a wolfish expression.

"What's wrong, One-Arm? You look even more sulky tonight than usual."

"Maybe he's not satisfied with his prize," said Olbius, the fat-bellied chieftain from Mochios in the east.

He referred to the young woman who knelt at the foot of Amynias' couch, head-bowed, naked except for the fetters on her ankles and wrists—the daughter of a wealthy Rhodian family, now reduced to a slave. Amynias had been given his pick of the captives from Kamiros, behind only the eight chiefs and the skippers who carried out the raid.

"On the contrary," Amynias declared. "I find the gift most appealing. I intend to make vigorous use of her."

Several of the chieftains guffawed.

"Only Amynias could make bedding a wench sound like taking a cold bath!" Ephoros roared.

"To speak bluntly, my lords," Amynias said, "I wonder a little at your lack of urgency. You've made fine progress in planning your summer campaigns. But now your captains lie feasting while the Rhodian navy bears down on you."

"Oh, you heard about that, did you?" Ephoros said.

The news had arrived that morning in Plakatas, the port town where the pirates were gathered. A dispatch boat had run up on the beach after two days and nights of hard rowing. From the estimate Amynias had heard, the Rhodians had probably reached Crete yesterday.

"Don't worry, One-Arm" said Pittacus, another of the chiefs. "We've already discussed the matter. Six of us are taking our fleets out at dawn to meet the invaders."

"One-Arm has sailed with the Rhodians," Olbius pointed out. "Maybe we should take him along as an advisor."

Amynias responded with a mirthless smile. He deemed it critical never to show weakness to these men. "I'd be glad to join the expedition, if you feel my knowledge can be any help."

"Hah! You are as brazen as you are ruthless," Olbius cried. "That's why we regard you as our brother. But we know the Rhodians better than they know themselves. They send only twenty galleys, out of fear of leaving their coasts unprotected. Rest assured, we will rout them and be back to our feasting in just a few days."

Meat was served on heavy bronze trays. The chieftains attacked their dinners with knives and fingers, smearing their ribboned beards with grease. Amynias observed them quietly as he sampled a little beef and brown bread.

When much meat and wine had been consumed, a spearman came and whispered in Ephoros' ear. The chieftain brightened and scrambled to his feet.

"Here's another prize from Kamiros that might interest you, Amynias."

He lifted his chin toward the doors, where a pair of burly pirates dragged in a chained prisoner. As they neared the dais, Amynias saw that the bony captive was naked, his skin marked by bruises. Ephoros had stepped down from the dais. He drew his sword and pushed it carefully into the coals of a brazier.

"You look confused, Amynias. Don't you know your old messenger, Bolocrates?"

Hearing his name, Bolocrates raised his head. He seemed to recognize the chieftains, and his dull expression changed to one of panic. His cracked lips worked and his throat emitted a dry, wordless croaking.

"Sadly, he cannot say hello," Ephoros explained. "He's already been relieved of his tongue."

Staring at the man who had betrayed him, Amynias experienced divergent feelings: a black gratification that Bolocrates had been tortured, a queasy distaste at being forced to witness the result.

"Brothers! Brothers!" Ephoros shouted, until the entire hall grew still. "This man Bolocrates betrayed us. He is the knave who testified against our banker in Rhodos, causing the guild to lose many thousands of drachmas. It was only through Amynias' wise planning and cunning that we did not lose more."

Ephoros twisted his sword in the embers. "The punishment for traitors is blinding and hanging. By our law, any aggrieved shipmate can carry out the sentence. I offer this right to our brother Amynias One-Arm, who has suffered exile and confiscation of his wealth on our behalf."

Amynias' gut cringed. All eyes watched him expectantly. Grinning balefully, Ephoros held up the blade, gleaming red.

Amynias rose and circled the table. Inwardly, he cursed the brigands for putting him in this grisly position. But plainly, he had no choice. In their eyes, failure to carry out the sentence would cast doubt on his courage and trustworthiness. He received the sword from Ephoros and marched to the spot where Bolocrates waited, pinned immobile against a pillar by the two thick-armed pirates.

Whimpering, Bolocrates watched as the searing blade moved close. Amynias steeled his nerve and thrust the tip into the man's left eye. A gurgling cry escaped from the throat. The head jerked, and the eyeball sizzled and burst. Amynias pulled the bloody point free and pierced the other eyeball.

A savage roar of approval swept over the feast hall. Bolocrates slumped, unconscious. Amynias tossed the sword to the floor and stepped calmly back to his couch. He picked up his wine cup and sipped.

"Take Bolocrates out and hang him on the wall," Ephoros commanded. "So must all traitors end!"

"Well done, One-Arm." Olbius raised his cup in salute. "Now you are truly our brother."

The scrying bowl tilted in his lap with the steady rocking of the ship. Over his head a lantern swung on a creaking chain, its sputtering light reflected in the bowl. Breathing slowly, Korax peered into the stirred mixture of water and blood.

At his knee lay a hand-drawn map of Crete. For four days the flotilla had crept along the jagged coast. The Rhodians had discovered a few hemiolias hidden in coves and on beaches. They had burned the ships and nearby buildings, slain a few men who tried to interfere. Otherwise they had met no resistance.

But somewhere along the coast the pirate fleet lay waiting. Korax could sense them, but could not see where. Each night he strained to pierce the perceptual veils that hid the Cretan forces. Each night the veils grew darker and denser. The longer Korax spent at sea, the heavier grew Poseidon's immanent power. Now it suffocated him, smothering his courage and will.

He set down the bowl. His mouth was parched, his forehead hot with fever. The fevers were becoming more frequent and acute—the energy of Helios, un-discharged by magic, burning him up inside. Pain throbbed in his neck and behind his eyes. Korax squinted hopelessly at the map. At last, he struggled to his feet.

He needed air. He snuffed the lamp wick, opened his door, and moved down the gangway, leaning on the walls for support. Emerging in the cool night, he slumped to the rail on wobbly legs.

The ship lay quiet under a gibbous moon, the only noise the faint lapping of water on the hull. Shreds of mist drifted between the anchored fleet and the coast. Out to sea, banks of fog rolled and glimmered in the moonlight.

An officer paced toward him, armed with pike and shield. Peering at the face, Korax recognized Cimon.

"Are you sick?" Cimon asked.

"No." His voice was hoarse. "I just wanted some air."

Cimon nodded, unconvinced. He gazed sternly at the low, dark coast. "May I ask if you've had any success?"

Korax shook his head.

"We'll be all right," Cimon declared. "Whether your gifts can aid us or not, we'll find the brigands and defeat them. Not that I don't commend you for volunteering to join us, I do. It was admirable."

"Thank you."

Cimon held silent for a while. "I never apologized—I mean for my involvement in Amynias' scheme. I wasn't at your trial, but I like to believe I too would have stood up and confessed, as Patrollos and Lyceas did. Anyway, I regret what we did to you, I hope you know that."

"You can set your mind at rest."

Cimon expelled a breath. "I appreciate it. We're all on the same side now. No reason we shouldn't be friends."

Korax gave a feeble laugh. "I wish Patrollos felt that way. I am betrothed to his sister, yet he can hardly bear my presence."

"Still, he put his reputation at risk for you—I mean, by advocating that the admiral bring you along."

"I admit it, he put his feelings aside for the good of Rhodes. But all his guilt and torment, he needs to put those aside as well."

"I agree with you," Cimon remarked. "I will tell him so."

Moments later, they both turned their heads as another man approached, a bulky figure in a plain chiton. Recognizing the admiral, Cimon snapped to attention. Korax did likewise.

"Gentlemen, be at ease."

With the admiral's permission, Cimon resumed his inspection of the deck watch. Nicocles leaned his forearms on the rail.

"The moonlight on the water is beautiful, isn't it? Sometimes the sea is so peaceful, it makes you forget the dangerous times." His eyes swiveled to catch Korax's glance. "When I have a command, I always get up every few hours to pace the decks. Otherwise I can't sleep at all. But what is your reason for being out so late?"

Korax swallowed, his throat raw. "To clear my head. My lord, I've still had no success in perceiving the pirates. I know they're waiting somewhere ..."

"Yes, they're out there for certain."

"I cannot see where. This happens sometimes with the scrying art. Things can be concealed. I'm afraid my skills may fail you."

Nicocles contemplated the quiet sea. "My friend, I have a wife and two daughters. Each time I go to sea, they fear for my safety. I always tell them they need not worry, that even if I am lost, Rhodes will protect them. And the Rhodians will always be able to protect them, because our island has the special aegis of Divine Helios. I tell them this because I believe it. I believe it, because believing anything else leads me to despair. I've always been skeptical that your soothsaying could help us. But when you came to me with your offer, I felt the hand of Helios had moved you. I don't know why the god sent you on this mission, but I always believe he has his reasons."

The admiral scrutinized Korax's face. "You look feverish again. Try to get some sleep."

Dark clouds glided low in a pale sky, driven by a stiff wind off the land. The Rhodian fleet sailed with the wind abeam, lookouts scanning the uneven, rocky coast for signs of hidden pirate craft. The warships moved in a tight v-formation, the *Epicherse* in the center, the two supply ships reaching behind her. In the morning they had passed the island of Dia to starboard, a dark mound on the edge of the gray sea.

Ahead, chalky cliffs rose over the beaches in a place where the coastline jutted north. As the ships veered on the wind, a trumpet wailed and alarm flags went up on the forward triremes. A line of hemiolas swarmed around the northern cape, coming on fast under oars. Even as the Rhodians scrambled to battle stations, a second force was spotted behind them, sweeping down from the northeast. This larger force must have anchored behind Dia and waited for the Rhodians to pass.

Korax snatched his pike and shield and raced through the chaos of the main deck to his assigned post. Leukon was already crouching at the rail with the other deck-fighters. The flagship pivoted beneath them as the flotilla turned to meet the attack. Scanning the sea, Korax realized the size of the pirate force: fifty ships at least, mostly hemiolias but also some triremes the Cretans had seized in sea fights.

Then another realization chilled Korax's blood: the assault had them cornered in the bow of the coastline. Here was the ambush Korax knew was coming but could not foresee. He could almost hear the sea-god's mocking laughter.

In a shiny cuirass and crested helm, Nicocles strode along the deck, shouting to rouse his troops. "You men sailed for the chance to avenge Kamiros. Now you have it. Stand ready to fight for Rhodes!"

Near Korax's place, men frantically hauled on lines to reef the sail. They had no time to lower the yard or unstep the mast. The galleys would have to go into battle with their rigging exposed. Already crewmen were cranking the ballistas, pointing their darts at the oncoming ships. The sharp, zooming noise of their first shots was quickly answered by a hail of pirate arrows clattering on the deck.

Korax hunched his shoulders behind his round shield.

"You've never been in battle before," Leukon observed. "You had better stick close to me."

The foremost Cretan vessels slowed, their rowers backing water. Having come within range, their skippers preferred to punish the enemy with their expert archers before engaging in ship-to-ship fighting.

In answer to a blare of trumpets, the Rhodians rowed furiously to the attack. Their higher decks, turrets and armored troops gave them an advantage in close combat. But because of the length of the Cretan line, the Rhodians were forced to spread their formation. Some pirate vessels slipped into the gaps, while others backed away. Volleys of arrows rained on the Rhodian decks and men fell, wounded and dying. The men of Rhodes answered with slings, javelins, and the deadly barbs of their artillery.

A hemiolia swept close to the rail of the flagship. An officer shouted the order and Korax and his companions reared up and flung javelins. Korax could see the wild, eager faces of the pirates across the water, and the blur of their arrows streaking in the air. He ducked just before the volley hit. The marine beside him slumped and rolled onto the deck, a feathered shaft protruding from his eye.

A shock thundered through the quinquereme, and Korax was nearly thrown off his feet. The flagship's bow had collided with another hemiolia. The cathead scraped the pirate's low wales. With oars drawn in the two vessels slid alongside. The Rhodian fighters ducked another wave of arrows as the Cretans flung grappling hooks and spanned the gap with boarding ladders. In moments they were swarming up the ladders, casting javelins and shooting arrows at close range. The Rhodians roared and met them at the rails, thrusting with pikes. Leukon heaved his pike into the fray and drew his long sword.

"Stay behind me," he shouted to Korax.

They closed on the enemy, Leukon hacking and thrusting with his blade, Korax a step behind, holding up his shield and jabbing with his pike. Marines from the other rail charged into the melee and Korax was pressed into a packed, surging mob of spear points, shields and screaming men. Buffeted, he slipped in some blood and fell backward. Flat on his back, he saw the Cretans giving way, retreating down their ladders, some jumping overboard. The Rhodians started to pursue, but their officers ordered them back.

Korax gained his feet amid piled corpses and gasping, wounded men. All around the sea was a tumult of galleys in close combat. The Rhodian formation was scattered and another wave of pirate ships was bearing down on the battle.

Nicocles strode the main deck, waving a sword and shouting. "Break off! Break it off! Raise the red. Blow the retreat!"

Trumpets sounded from the rear deck, and the red flag scurried up the mast, the signal to retreat. Nicocles wheeled and shouted orders to the helmsmen. Then an arrow pierced his neck and he fell.

Bent low, Korax clambered over the body-strewn deck, arrows dropping around him. Nicocles fought weakly to rise. Korax held up his shield to protect the admiral's head and used his free arm to roll the man over.

Nicocles retched, eyes wild, drowning in his blood. Korax managed to turn the admiral's shoulder, and Nicocles coughed and a stream of blood poured from his mouth.

"Get them away," he croaked. "North."

Korax looked around, appalled. Patrollos ran toward them and dropped to his knees.

"Commander." Nicocles recognized Patrollos and seized his arm. "Run north, wind behind you. Abandon the freight ships. Save as many as ..." His throat seized up with another fit of coughing.

"I understand, my lord." Patrollos turned to Korax. "Stay with him." He lurched to his feet and rushed across the rolling deck toward the helm, bawling orders.

When Korax looked down again, Nicocles was dead.

The Rhodian warships heeded the signal from the *Epicherse*. Rowing hard, they disengaged from the fight and broke for the north. The pirates gave chase, harrying them with arrows. The Rhodians responded with slingers and ballista fire. Their yard-arms were still raised and now they dropped sail. The brisk wind swept them ahead of the pursuit. By the time the Cretans could step masts and unfurl sail, sixteen of the Rhodian galleys had escaped out of range of their arrows. Rowing at speed, the Rhodians increased the distance, and finally the pirates gave up the chase.

Chapter Twenty-Three

That night, the Rhodian ships floated close together under a starless sky. A few lamps burned on the decks, where weary crewmen sponged up blood and wrapped corpses in burial shrouds. Korax sat with his back to the rail, still clad in armor. Overcome with nausea and fatigue, he had vomited his supper. Now a chill sweat dampened his skin.

Leukon was off somewhere, helping to tend the dead and wounded. Gruesome howls sounded sporadically from below decks. Korax did not know if the screams came from prisoners being tortured for information or injured men having limbs sawed off.

"You do not look well." Cimon handed him a water skin. "Are you wounded?"

Korax shook his head. He had suffered only scrapes and bruises.

"Well, if you're fit enough, we're meeting with the surviving captains. Patrollos would like you there."

Korax tried to stand up and failed. Cimon lowered an arm and hauled him to his feet. They walked across the main deck and entered the officers' quarters, a relatively spacious cabin with bunks along the walls. Oil lamps flickered on a long table surrounded by grave, demoralized faces.

"He is Korax," Patrollos told the officers. "I think you all know Cimon."

The captains nodded stonily at the newcomers. Korax took a place in the background, leaning against a bulkhead.

"The situation is this," Patrollos began. "Our admiral is slain. Our two sub-commanders were stationed on ships that did not escape the battle, so they are either dead or prisoners. That leaves me the ranking officer."

The captains and officers must have known this already, for their half-lit faces showed a uniform lack of response.

"I will speak bluntly," Patrollos continued. "I am younger and less experienced than many of you. Before becoming Nicocles' second, I served only one year in command of a quadrireme. Some of you no doubt feel I received hasty promotion because of my illustrious family. But this is not the time or place for mulling over politics. I would not have wished to take this command, but it is mine, and I will do my duty. Now, I will hear your opinions of our status and recommendations for our course."

Some of the officers stared impassively. Others frowned at each other stubbornly.

"Come, gentlemen. Speak freely," Patrollos urged.

One of the younger captains cleared his throat. "Our status is that we are beaten. In my view the only sensible course is to return to Rhodes. This mission was a fool's errand from the start. Twenty galleys against the whole of Crete! After Karpathos, we ought to have known better. But apparently the Council has not yet learned to take the Cretans seriously."

"This mission is a punitive raid," an older, bald man answered belligerently. "As such, it has not failed. We inflicted respectable casualties on the pirates today, and we still have sixteen galleys."

"But not their full crews," a third man pointed out. "And we've lost our supply ships. We have enough food and water for two or three days at the most."

"We can replenish our food and water in Crete," the bald captain replied.

"And sail right into another trap?"

"There is another option," a gray-haired skipper commented. "There are uninhabited isles northwest of here where we can take on water. As for food, we can proceed on half-rations."

"With the men we have left," Patrollos said, "how many galleys can we man at full attack strength?"

Heads swiveled as they considered the question.

"Thirteen," someone said.

"Or fourteen," said another.

The discussion swayed back and forth. Feeling light-headed and sick, Korax strained to follow the arguments. Suddenly, Patrollos addressed him.

"Korax, Nicocles brought you on this voyage as a seer and advisor. What is your view?"

Stern faces confronted him, and he tried to collect his wits. He thought of his father, who had pleaded with him not to go on this voyage; of Thalia, who feared to lose both brother and future husband. How tempting it seemed to sail home, to return safely to the people he loved, to not have to face again the horrors he had witnessed today. But for all his wishing, he could not counsel retreat. Implacable duty would not allow it. The gods demanded a harder road.

"So far, I've failed you both as seer and advisor," he answered ruefully. "But I will keep trying. For what it's worth, I don't agree with giving up. The Rhodians sent us on this mission not only to punish the pirates, but to rescue the captives from Kamiros if we could. So long as there's a chance of that, we owe it to them to keep fighting."

The captains pondered his speech in silence. Finally, Patrollos spoke.

"I agree with Korax. Tomorrow we'll consolidate crews and supplies and sink the extra galleys. We'll sail northwest and take on water. We'll lick our wounds and plan a new attack."

Black spots danced in front of his eyes as Korax struggled to unlace his armor. Suddenly he bent over, retching. His empty stomach heaved, and he brought up a mouthful of bile. Still in the corselet, he rolled onto his bunk and blacked out.

He woke in the night with a raging fever, thirsting, too weak to rise. In the space above, the oil lamp drifted on its chain. Eventually, the oil ran out and he lay in utter darkness.

He dreamed he was drowning, sinking numbly into lightless depths. He would sink forever, for he was only a tiny thing, and the ocean was vast and bottomless. The ominous voice of Poseidon whispered triumphantly in his ear.

"You should not have ventured out on the sea."

He recalled Amynias, strangling him, taunting him that he should never have come back to Rhodes. Somehow, Poseidon and Amynias had become one and the same—the treacherous, tireless enemy who had defeated him at last.

Korax hung over the side of the bunk, coughing, spitting up dry mucous. Breathing was agony, his lungs scraped raw inside.

When next he woke it was day, gray light shining at the edge of the cabin shutters. Leukon sat over him, and Korax noticed his armor had been removed. He opened his mouth to speak, but Leukon pressed a bowl of water to his lips. Korax tried to swallow, but choked and spit it up. Leukon persisted until some of the water stayed down.

Korax passed out again. In his delirium, he relived the rite of the First Tower, when the sun god reached down to earth to swallow him. Now the god's power consumed him, a blaze too bright and searing for his mortal shell to bear. What insane arrogance had led him to think he could wield such power? The same pride that caused him, long ago, to invoke Dionysus to help him win a poetry contest. That time, his mother had rescued him from the destruction he brought on himself. In Alexandria, Miriam had saved him, and his mother's spirit had come in a dream and led him to Athene. He still wore Miriam's amulet on his chest, but its aura seemed weak, powerless, like Athene herself, to protect him out here on the sea.

Korax opened his eyes in the dark cabin. His groping fingers caressed the bed curtain, the tapestry of Thracian weave given him by his mother. He prayed to her and to the spirits of her grandmothers, to rescue him one more time with their magic.

He slept easier after that.

Eventually, Athene came to him in a dream. They stood together on the roof of her temple in Rhodos, the lovely city spread below, the Colossus shining nearby. Instead of a spear, she carried an olive branch that she brushed around his head to give her blessing.

"You have lost a battle, Korax of Rhodes, not the war."

"I cannot defy the sea god," he told her. "The power is in me, but I am too weak, too afraid."

"On land but not on the sea."

He had heard those words before, but when?

His eyes blinked open in daylight. Leukon held water to his lips and he swallowed. He wanted more, but the Celt told him he must wait.

"Your fever is broken. You will recover now."

"How long?"

"Two nights, one day. We've landed on an island. The ships are taking on fresh water."

Leukon gave him more to drink. Then Korax slept. At noon, he was awake and strong enough to eat some porridge.

The island was steep and tiny, a bare mountain peak jutting out of the deep sea. The Rhodian ships had sailed into a sheltered lagoon, the smaller galleys drawn up on the beach, the larger ones anchored in the shallows. The isle had no springs, but the mariners were able to replenish their water supply from pools of collected rain. Using planks and benches taken from the galleys they had abandoned, they built pyres on the narrow beach and held funeral rites for their dead.

The pyres were still burning when Korax emerged from his cabin. Weak, though much recovered, he picked his way down the long landing bridge that connected the quinquereme with the beach. He bathed in salt water, using a strigil to scrape away the foul effluvium of his sickness. Dressed in a clean chiton, he made his way along the beach past the smoking pyres.

Awnings were hung from the bow of a beached trireme, making a tent. Inside, Patrollos supped with his officers and captains. He had sent word, inviting Korax to attend if he felt well enough. Korax sat on a bench at the end of the long table. He ate lightly: bread, dried fruit, watered wine.

After supper, oil lamps and a chart were spread out on the table. Standing in his corselet, Patrollos drew his sword to use as a pointer.

"Gentlemen, it is time to decide our next action. From interrogating our prisoners, we believe that nearly the entire pirate fleet is anchored here, at the town of Plakatas, near the entrance to this bay the Cretans call Stilos. They sailed from this port to intercept us. The chiefs of their league were meeting there to plan their summer voyages. What is more, both of the brigands who talked claimed that the captives from Kamiros are being held in the town, pending ransom or sale to slavers. It would seem we've been given a rare opportunity, to catch their whole fleet in port and rescue our people. Opinions?"

"It sounds too convenient," one of the captains said. "The Cretans are famously hard to crack by torture. And they are crafty. Isn't it possible they were told to feed us this story if captured?"

"Possible, but unlikely," answered a grim, bearded marine. "Interrogating the prisoners was my distasteful duty. These two men divulged their information only after suffering much pain. I would have expected a deception to slip out of their mouths more readily. And I would have expected the same false story from the three others, who all died without talking."

"If the story is a ploy," said the bald, bellicose captain Korax remembered from the last conference, "that means the pirates will be waiting to trap us. If the story is true, they will still be on guard. So either way makes little difference."

"I agree." Patrollos nodded. "Gentlemen, I believe we must attack Plakatas. If the gods favor us, we will smash the pirate fleet and bring our citizens home. If not, we will trade our lives for as many pirates as we can destroy. Unless I hear convincing arguments to the contrary, this is my intention."

He looked from face to face. Some of the officers met his gaze and nodded fiercely. Others merely stared at the map.

"It is decided," Patrollos said. "The next question is how."

The bald captain jabbed with his finger. "Ideally, we should strike at dawn, using the brigands' own tactics."

"Surprising them will not be easy," said another skipper. "We can expect hemiolias patrolling the mouth of the bay, and watchmen posted on the headlands."

"That is correct." The marine who had interrogated the prisoners now pointed to the map. "We believe watches are posted on the cliff here and on this small island across from the town. Beacons burn at night to mark the channel for their ships."

"So if the night is overcast," Patrollos said, "we might be lucky enough to slip past the patrols and approach the beacons before we are seen. With the gods help, we could get within a mile of the town before the alarm is raised."

The captains stared dubiously at the map. Patrollos had put the best possible face on their prospects. If the entire pirate fleet was in Plakatas, the Rhodians would be outnumbered five to one, or worse. They would need complete surprise to have any chance of victory.

"Any way we could kill the watchmen?" someone asked.

"I don't see how," the marine officer said. "A ship approaching the island would surely be seen. As for the men on the headland, it is a sheer promontory to the point. The nearest landing we know is here, on the other side of the peninsula. If we landed a party there, they would have to climb over the mountains, with no known path."

"Not much point in taking that risk," Cimon commented. "The sentries on the island would raise the alarm in any case."

As he listened, an idea formed in Korax's mind, like colored threads weaving an image in a tapestry. "Suppose there were a fog, a dense fog low on the water? Your ships would be concealed, but still able to navigate by the beacon on the cliff. And if you rowed close to the cliff, you might not be seen by the watchmen on the island."

The men scowled, stared at the map, nodded appraisingly.

"You describe the perfect conditions for our raid," the bald captain remarked. He added in jest: "Can you conjure us up such a fog, soothsayer?"

On land but not on sea. The words passed like a whisper through Korax's brain, inciting a spark of power and dread.

"The weather is for the gods to choose," he answered, his gaze far away. "But I suggest that killing the watchmen on the cliff is worth trying. I ask that Leukon and I be given that mission."

"You? You are recovering from fever," Patrollos said. "I commend your bravery, but you are not fit for such duty."

"I will be fit enough in a day or two," Korax answered. "And Leukon is a prodigious fighter, raised in the mountains. Of all your company, he is probably the best man for such a mission. But he won't go without me."

His voice had grown firm and certain, his gaze locked on Patrollos.

"I will consider your suggestion," the commander allowed.

The discussion continued, revolving onto matters of rations and rowing shifts, the best time to disembark and best speed for crossing the sea.

Korax's thoughts drifted to the task he had set for himself—or that Fate had set. For now it felt predestined, the reason the god had prodded him to sail on this voyage. He believed he and Leukon could scale the cliffs and eliminate the watchmen. He even believed that his magic might stir the winds and raise the fog. But a premonition, dark and heavy, warned him he would pay for these accomplishments with his life.

The conference ended and the captains dispersed, returning to their vessels. As Korax paced along the beach, Patrollos walked up beside him.

"You seem much better. Yesterday, we doubted you would recover at all."

"I will be well enough for what I must do."

"You have something else in mind," Patrollos stated. "Something beyond killing the lookouts."

Korax said nothing, only stared at the sand as he walked.

"Do you think we have a chance?" Patrollos asked quietly. "It is hard for me to order these men to their doom. It will be a little easier if I believe we have a chance of victory."

Korax paused at the foot of the landing bridge leading back to the flagship. A giant full moon had risen, its light shimmering on the cove.

"As you said, commander, if the gods favor us, we will destroy the pirate fleet and bring our citizens home."

"Nicocles was right to bring you along," Patrollos affirmed. "Two nights ago, your speech inspired the courage of the others. I thank you for that. Whatever the gods decree, I am proud to have sailed with you, and proud to call you my friend."

He solemnly extended his hand. Korax clasped the thick-muscled forearm.

"I feel the same way, Patrollos. And I offer you this advice. Before you approach the bay, throw all of your water and supplies into the sea, as an offering to Poseidon. I do not know if we can appease the sea god and win him to our side, but it does no harm to try."

Patrollos laughed grimly. "Very well. There's no reason not to heed that advice. If we take the town, we'll find plenty of provisions. If not, we won't need any."

Chapter Twenty-Four

Black waves churned on the beach, turning ribbons of moonlight. The shallow penteconter groaned as its hull ran up on the shore. Crewmen dropped a landing plank, and Korax and Leukon scrambled over the side. Even as they trudged up on the gravel, men were pushing off with poles and oars were dipping into the water.

Korax carried his olive wand, sacred to Athene, instead of a spear. Herbs and magic gear were stashed in the pouch slung over his shoulder. Leukon bore a pike and a long quiver holding three javelins. Both men wore navy cloaks and boots and carried swords in baldrics.

As the penteconter backed water and put out to sea, Korax and Leukon marched along the beach in the gloom, looking for a path up the steep cliff-face. Normally, climbing in the dark would be folly, since any route could lead to a dead end. But Korax turned the question over to his intuition. The gods meant him to take this journey, so he trusted them to reveal the correct path.

He found a fissure in the cliff, where broken boulders spilled onto the beach. He looked up at the immense heights, framed against a misty sky illumined by the moon. After brief reflection, he hoisted himself up on the lowest tumbled boulder. Leukon grunted and followed.

They ascended for an hour or more, at times scrabbling on hands and knees, otherwise walking up steep, snaking trails. Finally, they came to a shelf that ended in a solid wall. The moon had moved behind the cliffs and Korax squinted around in the dark.

"We'll just have to wait for the daylight," Leukon said.

They dropped their gear and sat with their backs to the cliff wall. Neither man spoke, and soon Korax shut his eyes and dozed. He had slept fitfully since his fever broke, constantly alert, nerves on edge. He sensed the will of the sea god, pressing in on him, trying to pierce his resolve. Often, he imagined himself sinking into the dark and bottomless ocean.

"Korax!" Leukon poked him with an elbow. "You're muttering in your sleep."

"Oh ... My apologies."

"It doesn't bother me," the Celt said. "But at times like this, troubling dreams are best left behind."

Korax pondered the wisdom of that as the sky lightened.

At dawn, he could see they were perched on a dizzying height, high over the sea. The beach where they had landed was nowhere in sight. They breakfasted on dry bread and water, then retraced their steps. After a short distance, they reentered the fissure and Korax could see the beach below. Leukon pointed to another path that curled around the opposite cliff face. It appeared to lead inland and over the mountains.

But a gap as wide as Leukon was tall yawned between them and the trail.

"Can you make the jump?" Leukon asked.

Korax peered dubiously over the edge. If they failed, there would be no surviving the fall. He scanned the walls of the fissure above and below, looking for an alternate route. There appeared to be no choice.

"I'll go first," the Celt said. "Then you throw the gear."

Leukon backed two steps, took a running leap and flung himself into space. His tall body sailed over the chasm, and he landed crouching on the opposite ledge. Deliberately, Korax tossed their packs and weapons and Leukon caught them.

Korax uttered a quick prayer to Helios. He backed up, steeled himself and jumped. But in his weakened condition, his legs failed to lift him as high and far as he planned. For a terrifying moment, he thought he would not even reach the far side. His forward foot met the edge, and the ankle folded with excruciating pain. He would have fallen had not Leukon seized his arm and dragged him to safety.

Korax rolled on the ground, clutching his ankle.

"That is bad luck," Leukon declared.

He crouched and unlaced Korax's boot, then speculatively moved the foot. Korax hissed and twisted when the Celt's examination got too painful.

"Probably nothing is broken," Leukon muttered with a worried brow. "You'll have to walk as best you can."

He bound the ankle with a strip of cloth cut from his chiton, then pulled on the boot and laced it tight. Korax grimaced as he put weight on the foot. Leaning on his olive staff, he limped up the path.

The ankle throbbed steadily when he walked, but when he had to climb it caused agony. Each time he was forced to lean on the foot while scaling the sheer places, he feared the ankle would buckle and he would slide off the mountain. Still, he had no choice but to endure the pain and go on.

Late in the morning they topped a steep rise and looked down on a magnificent view. White cliffs marched away to the end of the peninsula, rearing over a deep blue sea. Ahead, the ground sloped steadily to a bleached ridge lined against a cloudless sky. In another hour, they clambered over the ridge and looked down on Stilos Bay.

Far below and to the south, Korax spied the small island he remembered from the map. Across a narrow strait, the pirates' village nestled in a fold of the coast. Hovels and small houses climbed the flank of a hill, with a stone castle perched at the crest. Scores of vessels lined the beach and rode at anchor in the shallows: hemiolias, triremes, coasters. Korax recognized two freighters and a trireme from the Rhodian flotilla—prizes captured in the battle. Tents and awnings were strung along the beach in front of the ships, sleeping quarters for the pirate crews too numerous to find lodging in the village.

Korax scanned the coast, but could not see the lookout station. He figured it must be below them, hidden by the shoulder of the mountain. Out to sea, he spotted three widely-spaced ships reaching along the horizon: hemiolias on patrol.

He and Leukon moved along the ridge away from the town, looking for a safe way to descend. The craggy heights stood bare of vegetation, so they needed a path out of sight. They searched nearly to the end of the headland, then doubled back, but saw no possible route.

Weak and exhausted, Korax sat down to rest while Leukon scouted the ridge toward the town. Night would fall in a few more hours. Unless they managed the descent before dark, they would be trapped on the cliff, unable to kill the watchmen. The Rhodian warships would sweep into the bay at dawn regardless. Korax wondered if he should forget the sentries and start working on the weather magic. But that would mean the fog he conjured would have to conceal the Rhodian ships from the sentries on the cliff as well as those on the island, while still allowing the flotilla to navigate along the headland. It seemed impossible.

Leukon crept back to the spot where Korax had stopped. "I found a way I think we can go down. It's a sheer drop in one or two places, so I'll need to lower you on a rope."

"Well, that might work if we had a rope," Korax said.

"Oh, we do." Leukon lifted the fold of his chiton. Instead of a belt he had a rope looped many times around his waist. "I borrowed this from the ship. I thought we might need it."

Despite his weariness and pain, Korax laughed.

A short time later, they clambered to the edge of a precipice. The way down was a crack in the cliff, with slight ledges and footholds visible on the otherwise vertical walls. The outthrust of the cliff hid the crevice from the town's line of sight. Leukon tied the rope tightly around his waist and Korax's.

The Celt went first, scrabbling nimbly down the wall. Korax followed the same route, moving with care. Twice they reached ledges overhanging precipitous drops. Both times, Leukon braced his feet against the ledge and fed the line through his hands, while Korax slipped down the cliff face, legs dangling in the air. When Korax was safely landed, the Celt would slide from the ledge and somehow clamber down the rock. Korax could only wonder at the man's agility and strength.

Finally they reached the base of the cliff, where piles of boulders cascaded down to the bay. Korax could see the upper parts of the town from here, but by dodging behind the larger rocks they could easily stay out of sight. A quarter mile in the opposite direction stood the lookout post, a steep crag with a flat ledge on top. A footpath curled along the headland, connecting the crag with the town.

Bent low, they started off toward the lookout post, keeping close to the cliff. As they drew near, Leukon pointed to a circle of rocks overlooking the spot where the path veered out onto the crag. From there they could spy on the lookouts and a stretch of the footpath. They crawled noiselessly to the hidden spot, then set down their gear.

After taking a quick look, Leukon dropped down beside Korax. "They will likely change the sentries at nightfall. Then I will go down and kill them."

"You mean we will," Korax whispered back.

Leukon shook his head. "Not with your ankle, Blackbird. Much better if I go alone."

Korax hated the idea of sending Leukon against two men, but he had to agree. In his condition, he would be of little help in a surprise attack.

He shut his eyes and waited, weak and dazed with fatigue. His neck ached, and he wondered if the fever was returning. He doggedly suppressed the thought. Any collapse in his health would have to wait till tomorrow.

At twilight, they heard footsteps and a muttering of voices. Leukon's hand closed on the haft of his pike, his eyes wide and gleaming. They listened as two men passed below them and greeted the sentries out on the crag.

The four men lingered together for a while, talking and laughing. Korax smelled smoke and heard the crackle of burning brush. He and Leukon peeked over the rock. The Cretans had lit the beacon fire and were standing around it, passing a wineskin. Finally, two of the brigands picked up their pikes and headed off down the trail.

Leukon gave them plenty of time to get out of earshot. By then, the last of the twilight was gone. Silently, the Celt set down his pike and drew his long sword from its sheath. Crouched low, he circled the rocks and stalked up the path.

Heart thumping, Korax peered down at the lookout post. One of the brigands sat by the fire. The other man stood holding his pike, staring out to sea.

Suddenly Leukon was on them, a darting shadow. The first man crumpled over, stabbed through the side. The other man turned, curious at the noise. He scarcely had time to tense before the long sword spitted his belly. Leukon caught the man's pike before it hit the ground. He set it down, then freed his sword. He dragged the body to the edge of the crag and tossed it over.

Korax gathered his gear and hobbled down to the footpath. By the time he reached the lookout post, Leukon had disposed of the second body and was tending the fire.

"Well done," Korax told him. He set down his pouch and olive wand and removed his baldric. "I will begin the rite at once. You understand: I must not be interrupted, no matter what happens."

Leukon merely nodded. He retrieved the rest of their gear from the hiding place then posted himself where he could watch the path.

Korax slid down before the fire and opened the pouch. He spread the scroll at his feet and read through the verses, which some member of the society of magicians in Alexandria had translated from the Babylonian:

The Means of Raising Fog for Concealment

The rite required the mage to surrender all sense of himself as a man, to become one with the fiery sun, with water and air. Stars sparkled overhead, but a hint of mist floated in the sky. Korax would need to thicken that moisture, to spread clouds to hide the moon and raise fog over the sea. He took dried herbs from his bag and sprinkled them into the fire. He breathed in the fumes and began to chant.

I walk in the ways of Utu the Sun
I walk in the secret places of the sky
Nammu of the watery deeps is my mother

I am gifted with the powers of An
My words spark the heat of the sun
My words are droplets of rain
My breath is the wind

I am Fire, Water, Air, and Mist

He repeated the last line over and over, and the power of Helios rose in his spirit. Gradually, it spiraled up his spine. Soon, its force lifted him out of his body. He flowed up into the cool black night, away from the fire and the rocks, soaring high over the island and the sea.

The sound of his chanting still droned in his ears, but far away, a distant murmur. He rode the upper currents, soaring like a raven or a hawk. After a time, he penetrated to a secret place, an upper realm where rain poured from pools and titanic bellows exhaled the winds. He sensed he could reach with his mind, as with feathery hands, to tip the pools and move the breezes.

But a sinister voice vibrated in his skull. "Who are you to seize the power of the gods?" Was it Poseidon, or Amynias?

Or was it the voice of his own inner fear?

If he succeeded in this working, he would likely die. He had realized that in a premonition, had already accepted it. He thrust the fear aside.

But now he was lost, drifting in a void. He looked in all directions but spied no light. The fear returned, stronger, smothering like a shroud. Air blew all around, but his breathing was tense and shallow.

Time passed, he did not know how long. Sometimes his eyes opened, saw a fire in front of him, saw Leukon adding logs and brush. Or did he imagine it?

He heard the chanting in his throat again, far away. He knew time was running out; he must get back to the sky's secret chamber. But each time he willed himself to rise, he sank again into the gloomy void, dragged down by fear and despair.

Who was he to seize the power of the gods?

What madness made him think he could conjure wind and fog? He was only a mortal, a fool. Again and again in his life, he had quested after knowledge and power—and failed to achieve what he intended. The whole course of his life had led him to this moment, this one crucial task. And now he was failing again. He was no great mage, no hero. He was only a man.

Suddenly, his feet touched the bottom of the abyss.

He was only a man—Korax of Rhodes. The gods had given him strange talents, blessed or cursed with an odd and winding fate. But, in the end, he was simply a man of Rhodes—like his father and the others of that generation. With their stubbornness and daring, they had defied the Breaker of Cities and preserved their freedom, had raised the Colossus and given a new sun to the world. In a curious way, that same task was now demanded of Korax—to draw down the power of the sun god, to wield it for Rhodes, to safeguard his people and protect their freedom. Perhaps he would fail. He might well lack the strength or skill to accomplish the task.

But he swore to all the gods that if he failed, it would *not* be because he lacked the stubbornness and daring proper to a man of Rhodes.

Deep in trance but with eyes wide open, Korax stood and limped to the edge of the crag. Under the full moon he faced the dark water and lifted the olive wand high.

I am Fire, Water, Air, and Mist
I am Fire, Water, Air, and Mist
I am Fire, Water, Air, and Mist

Breezes stirred. Dark clouds slid over the moon. On the black surface of the bay, strands of fog crawled like snakes.

Chapter Twenty-Five

Amynias arose at dawn, as was his habit. From his chamber in the castle tower, he glanced down on the village and the harbor. A wet wind blew from the north and heavy fog covered the wide bay.

Something about that fog struck him as peculiar.

Frowning, Amynias crossed the room and kicked the slave girl who slept at the foot of his bed. She whimpered and sat up, cringing. Amynias ordered her to help him dress, and she hurried to fetch a chiton and belt. Actually, Amynias' left hand was improving and he could, with effort, dress himself. But it was much easier to have a slave do it.

When the girl had finished lacing his boots, Amynias wandered outside. Descending the outer steps of the tower, he ambled along the parapet. He habitually took a long walk at dawn, usually feeling too alert and restless to sleep. And of course it was too early in the day to conduct business. The pirate chiefs and captains would be snoring for hours yet, most of them flopped on couches in the feast hall. For two days and nights they'd been drinking and carousing, celebrating their rout of the Rhodian fleet.

A sentry nodded as Amynias paced near him. "Good morning, captain." The man knew he was no captain of course, simply used the title out of respect. The Cretans were a simple-minded lot.

Amynias peered out over the water. With the dense fog he could not even see the small island across the channel. Strange. Yesterday had been so clear and dry.

"Curious fog this morning," he remarked.

"Oh, the weather's unpredictable this time of year," the sentry answered. "By noon it might be sunny."

Still, something in the atmosphere nagged at Amynias. He stared along the headland to where the lookout post floated above the fog. The watch fire still burned, at this distance a tiny spark. Odd how one of the lookouts seemed to be standing at the edge of the crag with his arms outstretched. And the second sentry was nowhere in sight. It probably meant nothing, yet the scene instilled a vague suspicion.

Amynias decided he would walk to the lookout post this morning. Prodded by instinct, he stopped at his room and armed himself with a sword and two javelins. He left the castle by a postern gate and started up the footpath with a vigorous stride.

At times, he passed through walls of fog so thick he could barely see the path below his feet. Then, as he neared the lookout post, he heard grunts and gasps and the clatter of weapons.

Amynias crouched low, the twin javelins clutched in his good hand as he stalked up the trail. Suddenly the mist parted and he saw combat.

Two Cretans with spears attacked a single, huge warrior. The tall man jabbed a pike with one hand and swung a long sword with the other. The Cretans were certainly two watchmen come to take the morning shift. But who was their foe? Abruptly, Amynias recognized him—the Celt, the henchman of his cousin Korax. Wildly, Amynias swung his head to regard the other man, the figure perched on the edge of the crag. At first, he could not be sure but then ... Yes! It was Korax.

Amynias lurched back against the rock face, hiding himself. His thoughts raced, trying to comprehend what he had seen. Somehow, Korax and his man had taken the lookout post. And now, while the Celt defended it, Korax was weaving some sorcery.

Amynias hefted the javelins, seized by a mad exhilaration. From the depths of his soul he longed for revenge, and now Fate had delivered Korax into his hands. If he could rush past the skirmishing men, reach his cousin on the crag, he might slay him before he ever turned around.

But as Amynias measured the distance, one of the Cretans went down. Pierced by the Celt's pike, he stumbled backward off the path and rolled over the cliff. The other man's spear stabbed the Celt deep in the thigh. The giant slumped, but smashed the haft aside with his long sword. He regained his feet, and the Cretan backed away fearfully. Sword leveled, the Celt limped toward him with a relentless, murderous aspect. Plainly, the second Cretan was about to die.

Amynias scanned the rocks above the lookout station. He let instinct make his decision. He left the path and picked his way over the rugged slope. As he climbed, he had to lay the javelins down on the rocks above, then hoist himself with his strong arm. He prayed grimly to the Fates that he would not be too late, that they had not shown him this chance only to pluck it away.

He clambered onto a boulder above the lookout crag. The Celt had finished off the second watchmen. He sat on the path, squeezing his thigh muscle, attempting to stanch the bleeding.

Then another movement caught Amynias' eye, a gliding motion down on the bay. He straightened and his mouth dropped open. Squadrons of warships streamed along the headland. The fog had parted so he could see them—and they could see the cliffs. But the dense fog still hovered elsewhere, hiding the swarming galleys from the island opposite and from the town.

Korax and his cursed sorcery!

Korax still stood on the edge of the crag, his hands sweeping slowly through the air. Amynias picked up a javelin and breathed deeply, letting the calm of a practiced thrower enter his body. The target stood well within his range, but he would only have two chances.

He raised the javelin, judging the distance with his eye.

Korax floated in a place of ecstasy. He saw the bay below him and the Rhodian ships flowing past. But he saw those things from the elevated perspective of a god. With his will, he moved the winds and shaped the cloudy walls of fog. The elements flew to do his bidding, like notes of music he plucked from a vast, golden lyre. This was the essence of magic, he thought, the perfect culmination of his art.

A swooping noise disturbed him. A thin shape flew darkly past his head. He blinked, thinking an arrow or javelin had just soared by. Dimly, he reflected that this was the price he had agreed to pay.

Had someone shouted his name?

A jolt struck between his shoulder blades. His arms heaved in reaction to a stabbing pain. He stumbled over the brink and fell toward the distant water.

Leukon was dragging the dead warrior across the top of the crag when he saw the first javelin fly. His head whirled to the boulders above. He spotted the man, and in an instant recognized him by his damaged left arm—Korax's cousin, the traitor. He was about to cast another spear.

"Down, Korax!" Leukon had time to do nothing except shout the warning.

But Korax seemed not to hear. The point struck below his shoulders, and he toppled over the cliff.

Leukon's spun, glared with killing lust at Amynias. The Celt drew his sword halfway from its scabbard, then growled and thrust it back. Staggering on his wounded leg, he hurried to the spot where Korax had gone over.

Below, the fog circled in the wake of the Rhodian ships. Leukon ripped off his cloak, dropped back two steps to gain momentum, then launched himself over the precipice.

By the time Amynias reached the ridge above the town, the fog had thinned and the attack was underway. The harbor was engulfed in flame and chaotic fighting. Rhodian galleys rode past the anchored pirate craft, dropping firepots from long poles to set them ablaze. Another wave of galleys rammed the hemiolias on the beach and fighters swarmed over the sides to engage the bewildered Cretans. Flaming missiles from Rhodian ballistas streaked through the sky, landing on the tents and huts of the pirate camp.

Chieftains and captains streamed in a ragged file from the main gate of the castle. Shouting in confusion, some still stumbling to pull on boots or armor, they rushed down the hill to organize a defense.

Observing them, Amynias concluded they were rushing to their deaths. The Cretan fighters in the town probably outnumbered the Rhodian force by five or six to one. But they had been caught completely off-guard. Sleepy, drunk, scrambling to find weapons, the pirates were being slaughtered.

Amynias knew he must act quickly if he hoped to escape. He hurried down the path, entered the castle through the unguarded postern gate, ran to his apartment. He commanded his slave girl to pack up his few personal effects and meet him in the main hall. He ordered his manservant to the stables to seize donkeys and load whatever provisions he could find.

After slapping the man's head for emphasis, Amynias armed himself with a spear and hurried away. He descended the curling steps of the tower, to an underground passage below the level of the feast hall. As he expected, the watchmen had left their posts to go and join the fighting.

But as he rounded a corner of the torch-lit corridor, he spotted two Cretan warriors, hacking at a thick wooden door with hatchets. One of them whirled, recognized him and grinned.

"Ah, Amynias. Just the man I was hoping to see."

"Olbius. What do you mean, my lord?"

"Oh, I think you know what I mean, Amynias. I think we've reached the same conclusion. The guild is finished, but we don't have to be. This is the treasure room, and I believe you have a key."

Amynias hesitated, eyeing Olbius and his henchman, wondering if they would cut him down.

Olbius thrust out a hand impatiently. "Come, Amynias. There's plenty here for both of us. In fact, we can help each other. I have men at the stables packing donkeys. I can help you get inland and hide out for a while. Then we'll go to the coast and ship out for some nice Aegean town, where you can help me invest my money."

He smiled roguishly, and Amynias found himself smiling in return.

An hour later, Amynias climbed a steep trail south of Plakatas. He followed Olbius and four of his men, each of them leading a donkey. The beasts carried water, provisions, and sacks of silver and gold taken from the guild's vault. Amynias had left his slaves behind, needing to travel light. Behind them and far below, smoke rose in billows from the burning town and the devastated pirate fleet.

Meeting Olbius had been a stroke of luck. The crafty chieftain knew Amynias' value and would make sure he survived. The pirates of Crete were finished, but with the treasure they'd stolen, Amynias would have ample opportunity to start again. And he could only be delighted with the gift Fate had brought him that morning—to finally have revenge on Korax.

Musing on these things, Amynias followed the pirates over the ridge and into the next valley.

Chapter Twenty-Six

Have I perished, goddess? Do you honor me with your presence in the Hall of Shades?"

Gray-eyed Athene smiled. "No, hero of Rhodes. Your road has many twists and turns, but it is far from over."

He floated as though in a pleasant bath. Then he realized the motion was the rocking of a ship. His eyes flicked open.

Leukon watched him. The drooping mustache made the Celt's grave expression almost comical. Korax chuckled—and immediately gasped in agony.

"Lie still," Leukon ordered. "The armor helped, but the point still broke two ribs and pricked a lung. Luckily, the salt water protected you from infection. Of course, hitting the water from that height could have easily broken your neck. You were lucky there again."

Korax remembered the fall and was amazed that he still lived. "Will I recover?"

"Oh, I certainly hope so! After I went to the trouble of jumping in after you."

Of course, Korax thought. How else could he have survived?

"Finding you in the sea was difficult enough," Leukon commented. "But keeping you afloat in that fog, when I could not see the shore—that was a heroic feat indeed."

Korax pressed his arm. "What a brave friend you are."

"Well, I had my reasons." Leukon's countenance grew serious. "It was your cousin who struck you down—Amynias."

Korax found the news surprising, but only at first. On reflection, it seemed an inevitable truth.

"I wanted to kill him for you." Leukon's tone was apologetic. "But I had to choose between that and saving you. Still, I imagine he perished when they burned the keep."

Korax searched his intuition. He slowly shook his head. "He's still alive somewhere. We're fated to meet again, I think."

Sometime later, Patrollos looked in on him. His face had a red gash and stitches where a sword had caught the cheek.

"My friend, I am so glad you are awake."

"Commander, my congratulations on your victory."

"The victory belongs to us all," Patrollos said. "And I am happy to tell you, it was complete. It will be many years before the brigands recover their strength, if ever. We took only moderate casualties, and were able to rescue three of our ships and their crews, as well as most of the people taken at Kamiros."

Patrollos seemed joyful in a way Korax had never seen, as if this victory had relieved the young commander at last of the torments that vexed his soul.

"That is wonderful." Korax smiled. "In a month, they will be singing paeans to you at the Salon of the Muses."

Patrollos compressed his lips. "We would never have survived the raid except for that fog. It was unbelievable the way it flowed around us, hiding our approach yet letting us see the coast. None of our skippers ever saw the like of it." He stared warily into Korax's eyes. "Perhaps it was because we made sacrifice to Poseidon, as you suggested. But I think our poets must praise the gods, for sending us such perfect concealment."

"So they should," Korax affirmed. "Definitely."

The town of Rhodos stretched under the sun on a brilliant spring morning. Hundreds of people lined the quays of the military harbor. Dressed in colorful finery, they waved and cheered as the victorious flotilla rowed into port.

Korax and Leukon stood together on the rail of the *Epicherse*, clad in their battle garb. Their pikes and bucklers rested at their feet. Korax was still too weak to lift the weapons, although his strength was slowly coming back. Leukon's wounded thigh was also healing nicely, though the Celt still walked with a noticeable limp.

"Isn't that a lovely view?" Korax surveyed the gleaming white town and the green hills.

"Rhodes is a comely land," Leukon agreed. "And that reminds me, I've been meaning to ask you something. You know that farmstead up in the hills that you got from your cousin?"

"Yes ..."

"Suppose I were to go up there with Kleis, and we acquired a couple of field hands. We could repair the house and the orchards, fix up the vineyards. By next summer we'd be growing grapes and apples. And your family would have a nice cottage in the hills, a place to escape the heat of the city. Does that not sound appealing?"

"Actually, it does," Korax admitted. "So you mean you want to settle up there with Kleis?"

"Why not?" Leukon demanded.

"Then, you're no longer planning to leave Rhodes? You're no longer concerned about the curse?"

"Oh, no. The curse is lifted. Didn't you realize?"

"I confess I did not."

"Well, you see, Rosmerta's curse required me to bring home the body of my brother. But now, I've done better." He set a hand on Korax's shoulder. "I've brought my brother home alive."

The final day of the midsummer festival was dedicated to Tyche as well as Helios. Priests read divinations in the temples, and soothsayers told fortunes in the marketplace. It was also deemed an auspicious day for weddings.

In the morning, Korax and Thalia made the rounds of the temples, offering sacrifices and receiving blessings on their marriage. Korax wore white ceremonial garb and carried a laurel staff. Thalia was bedecked in colorful raiment with a veil of sheer silk and a crown of pink roses. The bride and bridegroom had bathed that morning in water conveyed from a spring in an upland forest. The spring was sacred to the nymph Rhode, the bride of Helios who gave the island its name.

The banquet took place at the manor house of Philophron— such a feast as Rhodos had seldom seen. Hundreds of couches and festooned tables lined the terraces and porticoes. Members of all the ruling families mingled with naval officers, politicians, merchants, lawyers, and all the elite of the town. Zeno, Callipatria, and Leontes attended of course, along with Korax's cousins and their children. Staphylus was among the poets who sang in honor of the couple. Leukon shared a couch with Kleis, now a freedwoman and soon to become his wife.

But as he reclined on the central couch, Korax's eyes stayed mostly on golden-haired Thalia. She was a lively and beautiful young woman to be sure, and he had come to know and respect her character. But more than that, as he watched her laugh and easily converse with the illustrious wedding guests, she seemed to embody the very life of Rhodes, all of its virtue and richness—all that he had struggled to regain and then almost lost. Leukon had asked him once if the sun god kept his treasure in this island. The thought occurred to Korax now that this free and blessed life of Rhodes was indeed a treasure Helios bestowed.

At dusk, when the guests had taken their fill of meat and wine and sesame cakes, a carriage covered in garlands and drawn by white horses rolled up to the manor gate. Korax and Thalia climbed into the carriage, while Leukon the groomsman took the reins.

The procession moved slowly up the hill, the wedding party singing hymns. Thalia's mother Choronice led the way, carrying the bridal torch, with her tall husband Halitherses marching beside her. When the party reached Zeno's house, Zeno and Leontes opened the gates. Callipatria, standing in for Korax's mother, received the torch from Choronice and conducted the couple across the threshold.

Inside the house, the bride and groom were showered with nuts and dried figs, and Thalia was given a quince to eat. The couple retired upstairs to the bridal chamber, where Korax immediately barred the door. But the families and guests lingered late in the courtyard below, drinking and dancing and singing merry songs.

And that was the wedding of Korax and Thalia.

The night was warm and clear, a full moon painting the city with silvery light. Leaning on the rail of his balcony, Korax contemplated the harbor, a vague foreboding in his heart.

A rustling made him straighten and turn. Thalia crossed the balcony and handed him a cup. Her gray eyes watched him avidly as he tasted the sweet wine. She leaned against him, tilted her head and touched her lips to his.

"Will you come to me soon, dear husband?"

He smiled at her fondly. "Yes. I will."

Though they kept separate rooms, as was the custom for wealthy couples, Korax's chamber was now mainly a study. Nearly every night, his young wife invited him to her bed. She snuggled against him, then slipped away with a whisper.

"I will be waiting."

Korax watched her glide back through the lamplight. Sipping his wine, he turned and gazed down on the ships that packed the harbor. The trading season, now half-over, was already more profitable than any in recent years. Not a single pirate raid had been reported, and even the weather had been mostly fair. Korax did not know if the calm seas meant Poseidon was appeased by the sacrifices offered by the Rhodians, or if he had withdrawn to his palace in the deep to plot some new calamity.

"I believe he is appeased for now, though it is always hard to tell with my uncle."

The voice, as plain in the air as if spoken by a mortal, startled Korax so he almost dropped his cup.

"Hermes, god of magicians. You have returned to me?"

"I was never far away."

The voice blended the resonant tones of the Egyptian Thoth and the youthful, exuberant Hermes Korax had known in Alexandria. Korax closed his eyes and envisioned the speaker: the mature Hermes depicted on the most ancient statues, the smiling, bearded god, the protector of boundaries and roads.

"Does this mean Athene is no longer my ally?"

"Athene will come when you need her or when she has a task for you. All gods and goddesses are always within your reach, for we dwell in the depths of your soul. That is the nature of the gods."

Indeed. So Korax had gradually come to suspect.

"So, conjurer of Rhodes, it appears you have attained all your aspirations. You are wealthy and respected, a hero and leading citizen of your city. You have family, friends, a fair young bride who adores you. And yet, you do not seem content."

"Because I am uneasy … Because it all feels too perfect, and I know it cannot last." Korax watched the moonlight shimmer and change on the sea. "If there is one thing I have learned from all my studies, oh god of magicians, it is that all conditions soon pass away."

"A bitter truth, is it not?"

"Yes." Korax pondered the mystery for a long moment. Paradoxically, his mood brightened.

"And yet, not entirely bitter?"

"No," Korax agreed. "Because I know that Zeus will send the rains again in the winter, and Dionysus will come in the spring. He will bring the flowers and the new wine, and—assuming I still live—I will relish those gifts. And for now, well, Helios stands guard over Rhodes, and there is peace and freedom on the sea. The wine is sweet, and the young bride is sweet, and the summer nights of Rhodos are lovely indeed."

"So then you *are* content?"

Korax lifted his cup in a wry salute. "As content as mortal can ever be. No doubt, the gods will have trials for me in the future. But I will face them as best I can. In the meantime, I mean to enjoy my blessings while they last."

"Well spoken," Hermes concluded. "And that is wisdom."

Afterword

The *Conjurer of Rhodes* books are set in the 3rd Century BCE. I call this "the time of the Seven Wonders of the Ancient World" because, for a relatively brief period during that century, six of the historical Seven Wonders actually existed in the world. (The Hanging Gardens of Babylon had already passed into legend.)

This was a time of disruption. The short-lived empire of Alexander the Great had broken up into warring kingdoms, but the ideas of Greek culture had spread from the Mediterranean all the way to India. The result was frequent wars, unprecedented trade and cultural interchange, revolutionary movements in the arts, and wondrous advances in science and technology.

In other words, it was a lot like our own time.

The description and history of the Colossus of Rhodes in Chapter 7 is accurate according to ancient and modern sources. The giant statue of Helios toppled in an earthquake in 226 BCE. After consulting the oracle of Delphi, the Rhodians decided not to rebuild the Colossus, and its ruins remained where they lay until being melted down and sold by Arab conquerors in the Middle Ages. The true location of the statue is a matter of debate, although the popular notion that its legs spanned the entrance to the harbor of Rhodes is a medieval invention.

The account of Rhodes as a free state, its preeminence as a trading center, and its conflicts with Cretan pirates are all based on history. Remarkably, so is the story of the Celtic invasion of Greece as told by Leukon in Chapter 17.

As depicted in these novels, this was also a time of religious ferment. The Olympian deities of Greece were still worshipped, but gods of many lands intermingled, and new philosophies, both rational and mystical, flourished. As for the workings of magic in the world, and the intervention of the gods in human affairs—that. dear reader, you must judge for yourself.

§

As of this writing, the *Conjurer of Rhodes* titles are:

Book 1- *The Mazes of Magic*

Book 2 - *The Lights of Alexandria*

Book 3 - *The Treasure of the Sun God*

Korax has a long and winding fate. Whether more of his adventures will find publication is left for the future to reveal.

I am very grateful to my beta readers, John W. Kelly, Richard Fisher, David Wilson, and Nadia Castro. Thanks also to my fantastic editor Jaime Henriquez, and talented cover designer, Mirna Gilman of BooksGoSocial.

If you enjoyed this story, please consider leaving a rating and review on Amazon, as well as other sites. The algorithms of the publishing business make this extremely important to a book's success.

I love hearing from readers. You can connect with me at:

Web: triskelionbooks.com or jackmassa.com

Facebook: www.facebook.com/AuthorJackMassa/

X/Twitter: @JackMassa2

www.ingramcontent.com/pod-product-compliance
Lightning Source LLC
Chambersburg PA
CBHW020833260626
47169CB00003B/971